MW01702829

Praise for Anne Whitfield's *Long Distance Love*

"Anne Whitfield has written a very poignant story of two people from opposite ends of the earth, with opposite goals in their lives who fall in love... The love scenes are romantic and sensual. There are no boring moments in this captivating story and the reader will sigh at its satisfying ending. This reviewer would love to read more from Anne Whitfield."

~ *Valerie, Love Romance*

Sensuality Rating: Sensuous "Long Distance Love is a sweet love story that shows how two people in love have to work to stay together! I love how real it is... Long Distance Love is superbly written, genuinely romantic, and is a must read for anyone who finds true love irresistible!"

~ *Lindsey Ann Denson, Ecataromance.com*

"Long Distance Love is a most remarkable read. The style of writing is exquisite. Anne Whitfield writes stories that touch the heart. She is an incredible writer who takes believable challenging characters and spins tales that get better like fine wine and I believe this is an extraordinary read."

~ *Cherokee, Reviewer for Coffee Time Romance*

“Anne Whitfield's LONG DISTANCE LOVE is a very sweet romance that is truly a pleasure to read. Patrick and Fleur make a perfect couple. I loved watching their relationship develop. ...I love that Ms. Whitfield uses the local dialect throughout the story, it adds to the authenticity of the tale and gives it an old world feel. This is the perfect feel good story and I'd definitely recommend it.”

~ *Chrissy Dionne, Romance Junkies*

“I liked this book immediately. Fleur was a warm and lovable character, while Patrick was sexy and supportive with a lot of charisma. As a frequent visitor to Whitby, I enjoyed reading the romance between Fleur and Patrick against familiar backdrops such as the moors and the abbey. The 'stranger in a strange land' genre has a lot of appeal and this is an excellent example. I only have one question the next time I'm in Whitby, where can I find Donnelly's restaurant?!”

~ *Autiotalo, Enchanted Ramblings*

“Long Distance Love by Anne Whitfield is a Traditional Romance with love, lust, loneliness and pathos as Fleur Stanthrope and Patrick Donnelly struggle to maintain their long distance relationship. Even e-mail and telephone calls can't keep these two from missing each other. There are different time zones and cultural differences that get in the way of their burning romance.”

~ *JoEllen Conger - GottaWrite Network*

Long Distance Love

Anne Whitfield

A Samhain Publishing, Ltd. publication.

Samhain Publishing, Ltd.
512 Forest Lake Drive
Warner Robins, GA 31093
www.samhainpublishing.com

Long Distance Love

Print ISBN: 1-59998-571-3
Digital ISBN: 1-59998-023-1

Editing by Sasha Knight
Cover by Scott Carpenter

First Samhain Publishing, Ltd. electronic publication: February 2006
First Samhain Publishing, Ltd. print publication: May 2007

Dedication

Dedicated to my best friend Samantha Charlesworth, who made my three years in England an experience I'll never forget.

We may live thousands of miles apart now, but she still makes me laugh.

Chapter One

Fleur hitched the cardboard box onto her hip and with her free hand closed the boot. With a critical eye, she peered at the car's white paintwork. There was a small rust spot close to the rear right-hand brake light. She had missed that in her inspection at the dealer's lot.

Well, what did she expect when buying a secondhand car that was nearly as old as she was? For a moment she was annoyed with herself and hoped that the car didn't have any other unseen problems. Cars weren't her thing. That's what fathers and brothers do—the car thing.

They'd be exasperated by her eagerness to buy the car, any car, and start her adventure. Such impatience had ridden roughshod over her usual meticulousness. It was her attention to detail that had kept her well and safe on her many travels around the world. She might be impulsive but she wasn't a fool—normally.

Oh well, what's done is done.

Shrugging, she turned for the back door leading to the shop while jingling her keys to find the right one. She jumped as a tiger-striped cat leapt out from behind a garbage bin and disappeared over the fence. Pausing, she gazed around the small courtyard. Dirty concrete, broken lattice dividers between shop yards and several rubbish bins was not the welcome she had envisioned.

Still, that's what you get when you make decisions based only on Internet information.

Her family had been alarmed and dubious of her intentions, but, after all, they were used to her sudden announcements of her desire to tour some unknown country. This—moving to the opposite side of the world, buying an old car and opening up a shop for the summer—was typical of her waywardness and nomadic lifestyle.

Fleur unlocked the back door and pushed it open. A wave of staleness hit her. Dust mites floated in the evening sun that streamed through the little square window over the shop's small kitchenette. This rear area of the shop also held a tiny storage room, more of a cupboard actually. She poked her head around the dividing wall and into the shop itself. In the dimness, she made out the light pink painted walls and smiled. She itched to redecorate.

"One thing at a time," she whispered in the silence.

From the kitchenette, a flight of steep narrow stairs went up to the flat above. Fleur held the box to one side so she could see better, and eagerly went up to inspect her new home. Again the smell of mustiness tickled her nose as she opened the door.

After placing the box on the sitting-room floor, she examined the compact bathroom and opened the narrow window there to let in fresh air.

In the only bedroom, she unlatched the large window and opened it too. Leaning out, she grinned at the green window box and anticipated how it would look full of the pansies she planned to buy.

Below, a car crawled by at walking pace, obviously unfamiliar with Whitby's tapered cobbled streets. Fleur gazed up the street, which climbed sharply. Rows of centuries-old houses and shops lined the road like guards of honor. History seeped from every corner and she loved it. It was all so different from home. She knew this summer was going to be different, special. She couldn't wait for it to begin. An exciting and refreshing time after the awful couple of years she'd had recently. But that was the past and not to be thought of now, today. She felt good, totally revitalized and that's all that mattered.

Fleur skipped downstairs and out to her car to the boxes waiting for her on the backseat. Giddiness rose in her, she was as energized as a kid on Christmas morning. Her new life would begin now.

In her pocket, her mobile phone jingled with the tune of a Robbie Williams song. Her brother, Charlie, had put it on there for her going-away present. "Hello?"

"Fleur? Darling, how are you?"

At her mother's loving greeting, homesickness hit her unexpectedly. This shocked her. She'd only been gone two days, she shouldn't be homesick yet. No. It wasn't homesickness. It was, perhaps, guilt.

Despite their loving relationship, her mother hadn't understood her need to run off this time. "I'm fine, Mum. I just arrived at the shop. Yes, I picked up the keys. I'm unloading the car as we speak."

As her mother flooded her with questions, Fleur opened the car door and, one-handed, grabbed a large bag. "Yes, tell Dad not to worry, the car is sound even though it was cheap." If she'd had fingers free she would've crossed them.

Fleur walked back into the kitchenette and through into the shop itself. She looked around the empty space as her mother plied her with advice. "It will be okay, Mum. The shop needs redecorating but I knew that. I'll make a start on it over the weekend. The delivery truck should be here soon with my furniture... No, you don't need to come over. The airfare is too expensive. I can do this by myself. Yes, I'll ring Aunt Sal next week when I have time..."

Fleur walked to the large front windows. They needed cleaning.

"Mum, don't waste your money on phoning this mobile. I'll ring you tomorrow when the phone in the flat is connected, okay? Yes, I will be careful. Give Dad and Charlie a hug from me. Yep, I will lock the doors at night. Bye, Mum, love you."

Fleur tucked the phone back into her pocket and reached up to unlock the shop's glass front door.

Stepping out onto the pavement, she turned and looked at the shop's frontage. The old signs from the previous tenant still proclaimed it to be an herbalist and health bar. Well, she'd soon have that changed. She bit her bottom lip to stop her smile from spreading. It was still hard to believe she was here.

Whitby. England.

Renting a shop and living out a dream.

Well, she deserved it. The last two years had been hell and she'd made a promise to herself that if she survived it she would live life to the fullest and that's exactly what she intended on doing. Not everyone understood her need to do this. A holiday, yes, they all agreed she deserved that, but a business? In another country? That they didn't comprehend even though she tried to explain until she was blue in the face. She wanted to get in touch with her ancestry, the way her parents and grandparents lived. To experience the English way of life.

Movement to her left caught her attention. A man strolled down the street towards her. Fleur blinked. He had his hands casually tucked into his jeans' pockets and he wore a plain white tee shirt that didn't hide his wide shoulders and flat stomach. Her heart skipped a beat. *Boy, he's rather delicious.*

He paused a few feet away and glanced into the empty shop. "Hi. Just moving in?"

Fleur's stomach flipped at the sound of his soft Irish accent. His hair, dark and overlong, appeared windblown, as though he had just been walking along the beach, and she had a crazy urge to slip her fingers through it. She clenched them into fists to stop them from moving on their own volition. His lazy smile made the fine lines crinkle at the corners of his soft blue eyes. He had even white teeth and a touch of stubble covered his chin.

She stared dumbstruck. He was like something out of a menswear catalog.

Her very own model-type welcome party.

Could her day get any better? A delicious heat tingled throughout her body as he gazed at her. It was hard to think straight, but she managed to get the words out. "Yes, I moved in today."

"I'm Patrick Donnelly. I own the restaurant up the hill on the corner." He held his hand out and she slipped her hand into his. A solid, comforting warmth shivered up her arm making her feel very safe, protected.

"I'm Fleur Stanthorpe."

"You sound Australian?"

She raised her eyebrows. "Is that allowed here?"

"Well, being an interloper myself, I'll let you in on a secret." He leaned closer and his light cologne teased her nose, making her wonder at what the scent hinted at, but more shockingly she wanted to inch closer to smell him properly. "The people here are warm and friendly, but they'll gossip about you." He winked and straightened. "You'll be known as the Australian who owns the...?"

"Bookshop café."

"Café?" He stepped back and assessed her. "You cook?"

"I'm not a chef by anyone's standards, but I can make a mean pastry. I took a course in baking." Fleur tilted her head and smiled. His answering grin took away all coherent speech. She tucked a strand of hair behind her ear and hoped she looked presentable. She resisted the urge to glance down at her shirt. Spilling food and her generous breasts catching it was a common family joke about her. Unknown stains often appeared without her being aware. "So, you...you own a restaurant?"

He nodded. "Donnelly's." His gaze raked over her in a soft caress and she burned as though he had actually touched her. "Are you with family?"

"No. This is kind of a personal adventure."

"Sounds interesting."

Confused by this sudden raw attraction, Fleur stepped towards the door. She needed some distance from him and his powerful magnetism, which robbed her of her breath. "Well, it was nice to have met you, Patrick."

"You must come to the restaurant for dinner one night, on the house, of course."

"Um...sure, thank you. That would be nice."

A slow, warm smile lifted the corners of his mouth. "I'll hold you to that. We can't have visiting Australians reporting back that we don't feed you well here."

She breathed in deeply to stabilize her rapid heartbeat and forced herself to act naturally, to smile and flirt, but all she could do was stare into his eyes as though hypnotized.

He tucked his hands back into his pockets. "I'm pleased to have met you, Fleur."

"Bye then." She ducked inside and closed the door. He continued down the road and she watched him, or more pointedly watched his tight backside, until he was gone from view.

"Oh, God." Her hands shook and she closed her eyes momentarily.

She suddenly realized how long it had been since she'd had sex or even looked at a guy in any way sexual. She groaned and slapped her hand to her forehead.

The last thing she wanted was to be sexually frustrated when she had so much she needed to focus on. Still, two years without a man was bound to affect her, now that she was in full health again.

A summer romance?

The thought was quickly rejected as soon as it arrived.

No. Definitely not.

She was here in England to spend the summer living and working as the English do, as her grandparents and parents had done before they immigrated to Australia. It was a last ditch effort to be carefree and single before returning home and, eventually, settling down. She'd promised her parents, especially her mum, that after this stay in England she would remain home in Australia and put her wanderlust to bed...for a time.

Fleur smiled as she thought of her family, and admitted that she missed them more on this trip than on any of her previous ones. She guessed it was because the last two, *very trying*, years had brought them closer, and she knew her need to travel again had dismayed her parents. Hence her promise that this would be the last swan song of her regular disappearing act.

Someone walked past the shop window and Fleur nearly broke her neck trying to see who it was, or more importantly to see if it was the gorgeous Irishman coming back. Disappointment washed over her when she saw it was only an elderly woman pulling her shopping along in a green trolley.

Her mind came alive with the image of Patrick Donnelly. His cute grin, jaw-dropping good looks and great backside. For a moment she allowed herself to fantasize about him actually holding her, kissing her. Heat pumped through her like an electric current.

It had been so long since she felt attractive and the lovely Irishman had certainly looked at her as if he acknowledged the spark between them. *Or had he?* Was it all in her head? Perhaps she had imagined the signals flashing in his eyes?

She chewed her bottom lip. "Come on, Fleur, stop acting like an idiot. He's most probably married or gay anyway."

Taking a deep breath, she pushed away from the door.

Patrick leaned against the rail and gazed at the boats riding at anchor without really seeing them. Few people strolled about, a couple ambled along the shoreline and two children walked by licking violently bright-colored ice creams. He wouldn't mind an ice cream himself actually.

Seagulls whirled above his head, crying out, eyeing for an easy snatch of someone's chips when they weren't looking. A small breeze lifted the hair at his nape, but it wasn't cold. Thankfully.

He hated being cold.

Summer was coming.

And an Australian was in town. Interesting.

He crossed his arms against his chest and sighed deeply. Suddenly he remembered his friend, Declan, saying that five years was too long to be without a woman. That night in the pub, only a few months ago, his mates had laid bets on what kind of woman it would take to get Patrick back into the dating game.

Well, they had lost their money. All of them.

No one had picked a honey blonde Australian who was opening a bookshop café. A curvy, striking woman, with soft hazel eyes and a smile that made him forget his name.

Patrick had scooped the prize.

He looked down at his watch, 2:20 p.m., Thursday the twelfth of May.

The date and time he had stepped back into the land of the living again.

Chapter Two

Fleur flopped onto the lounge and yawned. Muscles ached that she never knew existed. She gazed around the flat.

The evening sun showered the room with a golden glow. The few pieces of secondhand furniture she bought on first arriving in Whitby added a little atmosphere, but largely the room remained sparse. She needed to put pictures on the wall, flowers in vases and rugs on the floor.

In time it would be as she wished, but first she had cleaned and cleaned and then cleaned some more. First the flat and then the shop. The weekend had flown by in a haze of mops, buckets and detergent.

"Yoo-hoo. Anyone home?"

A visitor? Fleur jumped up and ran down the stairs to the kitchenette. Apart from buying a few staples at the supermarket, she'd not been anywhere or met anyone since the encounter with the Irishman on Friday, which later that night came back to taunt her with a vivid dream that left her body hot and pulsing with need.

As if I need that kind of distraction.

A young, thin woman with a small child of about five years of age stood at the back door, which was open to let a breeze through into the shop to dispel the odor of disinfectant.

Fleur smiled. “Hi. Can I help you?”

“Hi. I’m Rachel Jones and this is my daughter, Courtney. We live in the upstairs flat next door. I just wanted to say welcome.” She had cheeky brown eyes, a crooked grin and looked to be in her late twenties.

“Thank you very much.” Fleur glanced from mother to daughter, immediately liking what she saw. “Would you like to come in?”

“Oh, we wouldn’t want to intrude,” Rachel said and patted Courtney’s hand she held.

“Really, it’s fine.” Fleur waved them in and led them into the shop itself. “Just excuse the mess. I’ve spent the last two days washing walls.”

“Urgh! What a pain for you.” Rachel smiled in sympathy and looked around. “We only just got back from my parents. We usually spend the weekends there. I’m glad you’ve moved in. I hated the shop and flat being empty. Kids tend to think they can run riot with spray cans when there’s a shop empty. Thankfully, it hasn’t happened yet, but it would’ve only been a matter of time.”

“Would you like to come upstairs and have a cup of tea or coffee?”

“Are you sure we’re not interrupting?”

“Lord, no. I’m finished for today anyway. I’ve done nothing but clean since I arrived. I could do with the break.”

“Okay then, thanks.” Rachel followed her to the rooms above.

“Have you lived next door for long?” Fleur switched on the kettle and got out cups from the cupboard.

"Not too long, about a year." Rachel settled Courtney onto the chair at the breakfast table, which divided the tiny kitchen from the main room.

They talked a little about Whitby while Fleur made the coffee. She poured Courtney a glass of milk and with a wink, let her open the packet of chocolate biscuits while Rachel asked questions about Australia.

"What will you sell in the shop?" Rachel asked, watching her daughter spill crumbs. She automatically scooped them up and onto the plate before her.

"She's all right. A few crumbs won't hurt." Fleur sipped her coffee. "I'll be opening a bookshop that also serves coffee and cakes and that type of thing."

Rachel's eyes lit up. "Oh, brilliant. I'll be your best customer."

"Good to know." Fleur smiled and wiped a hand over her face.

Tiredness stung her eyes. Cleaning and jet lag weren't good partners. "Anyway, that's the plan I have. Right now it seems a pipe dream. I've so much to do first. I need to paint the shop, ring suppliers, hire equipment and rummage for secondhand books to sell. The list is endless and daunting."

"My uncle knows of a guy who owns a retail warehouse. You know the kind that hires out drink fridges to shops and all that."

"Really?" Fleur sat straighter, her tiredness abruptly gone. "I need one of those to sell cans and bottles of soft drink for those who don't want coffee or tea."

"I'll get you his number or better still I can take you there. Do you have a car? Is that yours out the back?"

"Yes, it is."

"How about I ring my uncle in the morning, would that suit?"

"You don't mind?"

"Not at all." Rachel cradled her coffee in both hands. "When do you start painting?"

"Tomorrow. I have the paint and everything all ready."

"Would you like some help?"

Fleur paused, her cup halfway to her lips, amazed at the generosity of this woman. "Are you sure you want to help? I can't pay you anything."

Rachel laughed. "Don't look like that. I don't want to be paid and I wouldn't offer if I didn't want to. After I've dropped Courtney off at school I'm free until three o'clock."

"Thank you." Fleur grinned. "You're very kind."

"Well, to be honest I tend to get bored in my poky flat by myself."

"You don't work?"

"I did part-time until just recently." Rachel stood and took her cup and Courtney's glass to the kitchen sink. "Come along, my little cherub. Time for home and bath."

Fleur walked with them downstairs and they stood out in the yard. She tousled Courtney's light brown curls. "Thank you for staying for a cup of tea. I've enjoyed your company."

Courtney smiled shyly and Rachel rolled her eyes. "First time she's been lost for words for a while. It won't be long though, before she's bothering you to death."

"Oh, I'm sure we'll be great friends." Fleur glanced at Rachel. "Thank you for stopping by. I'm so glad you did."

Rachel blushed. "Me too. It's nice to have a woman here." She ushered Courtney to their own staircase, which ran from the yard up to their flat. "See you tomorrow. If there's anything you need, just knock."

"Thanks." Fleur waved to Courtney and walked back inside.

Standing in the shop, she inspected the drying walls. Movement at the large front window caught her eye. The Irishman, Patrick Donnelly stopped and lifted a hand in acknowledgement. Her heart fluttered wildly as she raised her hand in reply. Slowly, nervously, she pulled back the bolt on the front door and opened it. She smiled. "Hello again."

"How's it coming along?"

"Good." She waved absently behind her. "Scrubbing mostly."

His blue-eyed gaze took her breath away. Her body suddenly became alert to every one of her senses. She had an insane urge to run her hands over his chest beneath the navy shirt he wore. His chest would be hard and smooth she knew. Hazily, she noted how fresh and smart he looked. His casual clothes were of good quality, fitting his lean body well. God he was gorgeous.

"Miss Stanthorpe?"

Her gaze flew to his. Heat suffused her cheeks. She had been so absorbed in looking him over she'd missed his question. If only the ground would open up and swallow her. "I'm...I'm sorry?"

"I said that if cleaning is all you've been doing, you'd be hungry. Unless, of course, you're one of those females who doesn't eat meals?"

"Oh, no, I eat. A lot. I could never be a model. All that lettuce and water. No, give me puddings and chocolate, big roast dinners and I'm your girl!" She laughed like a fool, then, realizing what a spectacle she was making, clamped her hand over her mouth to stop herself from uttering another word. *Heavens. He must think I'm a complete fruit-loop.*

"Good. Then I'll expect you around about seven-thirty?"

"Tonight?"

He nodded, his smile slipping, no doubt at her strange behavior. "There's no pressure. If you don't want to, then that's fine."

Her smile was forced as his eyes revealed new reluctance. Obviously, he was wishing he'd never asked her and could she blame him? She took a deep breath. Suddenly, having dinner in his restaurant was something she very much wanted and it had nothing to do with the food. "I'd like to, if you don't mind."

He stepped back and nodded again. "Fine. See you then."

Fleur dived into the shop and slammed the door. "Oh my God." Where were her brains? She was twenty-nine-years-old and acting like a silly sixteen-year-old. What must he think of her?

She heard knocking coming from the backroom and pulled herself away from the door. "I'm coming."

"It's only me." Rachel popped her head around the wall into the shop.

"Hi."

"I wondered if you wanted to share dinner with me and Courtney? It's not anything fancy. Chops and a few veggies."

Fleur relaxed her shoulders, desperately trying to forget her embarrassing meeting with the Irishman. "I really would love to, but I'm having dinner at Donnelly's."

Rachel's eyebrows shot up. "Donnelly's? Woo hoo, aren't you the lucky one."

"Why?" Fleur frowned.

"Well, it's the poshest place to eat on the whole district. And the owner is the most attractive man in the district." Rachel sighed dreamily. "It's also the most expensive place to eat. That's why I've never gone." She winked.

Fleur traced the floor's pattern with the point of her sandal. "The owner introduced himself and invited me."

"Really?" Rachel grinned. "I've not heard of him doing that before."

Unsure now, Fleur faltered. "Perhaps I shouldn't go."

"Nonsense." Rachel folded her arms. "You have to go now and then tell me all about it tomorrow. It'll pass the time as we paint."

Fleur laughed. "Yes, I suppose so."

"What are you wearing?"

Groaning, Fleur slapped her forehead. "I have no idea. Come up and help me choose."

Rachel glanced back to where Courtney played out in the yard, trying to catch the elusive cat. "Courtney, we're going up to Fleur's flat. Come and help us pick out something pretty for her to wear."

Upstairs in the bedroom, Rachel and Courtney sat on the bed expectantly while Fleur opened her wardrobe and screwed her face up in distress. "I have nothing to wear. I packed lightly. I'm here to live and work, not to party every weekend. I've done my fair share of that in the last decade."

"A little entertainment isn't bad, surely?" Rachel chuckled.

Shrugging, Fleur flipped through a few garments. In the last two years she had been forced to curtail her exuberance for partying all weekend, and she'd found it wasn't so bad to use the weekends to do other things instead of recovering from hangovers.

"What about those black slacks?" Rachel pointed.

Fleur took out the tailored pants. "I could wear these with that gold jacket?"

Rachel shook her head. "Too dressy. Lord, I thought you said you'd packed lightly? This lot is more than I've ever owned." She stood and rifled through the wardrobe. "Ah, now this is nice." She pulled out a knee-length dress of shimmering silver silk. "This is beautiful. You'd look stunning in this with your hazel green eyes and your Aussie tan."

"It's one of my favorites." Fleur touched the smooth coolness of the material. "I have a mohair white wrap that goes with it."

"Wear them. You'll knock Donnelly's socks off."

"That's not my intention."

"No?" Rachel was incredulous. "Well, it should be. I would, given half the chance." She covered Courtney's ears and laughed. "Imagine *doing it* with him?" She fell back on the bed giggling. "How perfect would that be? He has the sexiest smile."

Fleur couldn't help but laugh. She completely agreed. "You are bad, Rachel Jones."

"No, sadly I'm not, but I'd like to be."

They laughed again and Fleur tickled Courtney's tummy.

Fleur hesitated, then, straightening her shoulders, pushed at the restaurant's front door, which opened easily at her touch.

She stopped and stared. Antiques, soft music, muted lighting, Victorian period landscapes framed in gold leaf hung on burgundy-papered walls, gold fittings and thick red carpet. The history buff within her sighed in pure pleasure.

The foyer's old world décor relaxed the butterflies in her tummy a little. She always felt at home within an atmosphere of classic elegance, much more than she did in the cold, sterile look of modern interior designs. It amazed her how glad she was that his restaurant was so totally to her taste.

"Good evening." The waitress smiled. She was dressed in a short black dress with a gold badge denoting her name as Angela, above the gold embroidered Donnelly's.

"Hello. My name is Fleur Stanthorpe. Mr Donnelly invited me tonight."

"Oh, yes. Please follow me." Angela skimmed Fleur's outfit in rapid time before turning on her high heels and walking behind the carved wooden screen that hid most of the diners from the foyer.

Fleur looked down at the slinky dress, which Angela had inspected with narrowed eyes. Had she made a dreadful mistake wearing the silver silk? She was in a seaside town after all, not London or Sydney. Taking a deep breath, she followed Angela's path through the elegantly laid tables.

Fleur sighed in relief when she noticed the other diners were dressed smartly. True, there were only five other tables in use and most of the occupants were over fifty, but still, she wasn't too overdressed, as she'd feared.

Out the corner of her eye, she searched for the handsome owner. Her skin tingled in anticipation of meeting him again.

What was she doing? An entanglement wouldn't do her any favors. Throughout the years of her traveling she had experienced many holiday romances, but that wasn't her aim this time. She needed to concentrate on the business and make it a success. That's why she was in Whitby—to live as a local, not to chat up gorgeous men.

"Is this table satisfactory?" Angela asked, pulling out the chair for Fleur.

"Yes, perfect. Thank you." She scanned the immaculate table setting.

"Is Mr. Donnelly joining you?"

"Oh no." Fleur shook her head and smiled, but something in the waitress' look made her smile slip slightly. "I'm on my own."

Angela inclined her head in a superior way. "Very good, madam."

Fleur took off her wrap.

"I'll take care of that for you." Angela grasped the item and, after a last disparaging look, disappeared.

What the hell was that all about?

Fleur sat and gently touched the flower decoration in the center of the table. The subtle sent of gardenias and blue lilies lingered. For a moment, sadness descended. Here she was at a beautiful restaurant, all dressed up and alone. To the other diners she must present a sad picture.

Normally, being on her own never bothered her. She often went to the movie cinema alone if no one wanted to see a movie she was interested in. She had backpacked to ten different countries by herself. So, why did tonight haunt and mock her? Since breaking up with her last boyfriend a few years ago, she'd been happily single. Besides, other things had taken center stage... She didn't need a man to make her content.

Sighing, she guessed her abrupt melancholy was because of the wake-up call she'd received two years ago. Time was ticking by. Was her biological clock a ticking time bomb about to go off? Fleur frowned. The thought surprised her. Marriage and children had never been high on her agenda to experience. Why was she thinking about it, then? Why was being alone suddenly an issue? Why wasn't she just enjoying being in a nice restaurant?

Fleur grunted softly. Self-doubt was disgusting and something she hardly ever did. Tiredness. That's what it was. She was jet-lagged and tired from cleaning. Swiftly, her mother's cautions came to mind. *Don't over do it, Fleur, remember what the doctors said.* Well, she was tired of doctors, tired of being well-behaved. For two years she'd done all that they asked.

"Miss Stanthorpe." Patrick Donnelly wound his way between tables towards her. Her breath caught. He looked magnificent. Black tailored trousers, shiny black shoes, a crisp white shirt, hair still damp from washing, and again that drift of soft cologne. Tonight he wore small gold-rimmed glasses and the effect was so sexy, so charismatic that it hit Fleur between the ribs like a physical blow. She wanted him and there was no denying it. Physical need circled and gripped her most inner core.

Fleur smiled, conscious that her heart had leapt crazily. "Hello."

"I'm glad you came."

"Thank you for inviting me." She couldn't take her eyes off him. "It's very kind of you."

"My pleasure." His lazy smile made her stomach clench and her breathing stop. "Actually, I was wondering if I could join you? I haven't eaten yet myself. Would you mind? Or do you prefer to be alone?"

"Of course, I wouldn't mind. Please do." Inside Fleur groaned. How on earth was she going to conduct a proper conversation with the man when her attraction to him took away all common sense?

Patrick sat down opposite and raised his hand to beckon a waiter standing near the bar. “Shall I order for us both? I have inside information.” He winked.

Fleur gripped the seat under her legs as her stomach cartwheeled. How was she going to eat sitting across from him? Oh why did all scrap of sophistication desert her now? “Yes, thank you.”

“The seafood is excellent, fresh today. What don’t you like?”

“Nothing, really. I love all kinds of food.”

His eyebrows rose. “That’s refreshing. Most women with a great figure like yours eat only salads.”

He said I had a great figure.

She took a deep breath and leaned forward, a smile dancing on her lips. “When I was growing up we didn’t dare not eat everything put before us. My parents hated finicky eaters. Now, I couldn’t deny myself something even if I wanted to.”

“Good. I’m not fond of finicky eaters myself. They’d put me out of business.” Patrick grinned and, looking up at the waiter, ordered their entrée first, creamy broccoli soup, and then asked for the wine list only to quickly change it to champagne. “Do you like champagne?”

Biting her lip, she shook her head. “I think I’m the only woman in the world not to, actually. Sorry.”

Amusement twinkled in his eyes. “Interesting. Okay. White or red wine?”

“White?”

The waiter, a young, good-looking guy, chuckled. “Dry, madam?”

Laughter rose in Fleur's chest. "I'd rather have something soft and fruity."

The waiter bowed, his expression fighting to be serious, and left them. Fleur knew what he was thinking, that she was all kinds of a fool. Who refused champagne? No one.

Patrick leaned back in his chair. "So, tell me, why is an Australian in Whitby?"

"Why is an Irishman in Whitby?" She grinned.

He shrugged. His face gave nothing away. "I wonder if your reasons are the same as mine."

"I doubt it." She looked away as more diners entered the restaurant.

"I'm hiding. What about you?"

She jerked around at his admission. Puzzled, she tilted her head to one side and studied him. "Hiding?"

Shifting in his chair, Patrick accepted the wine from the returned waiter and poured them each a glass. "Whitby is a good distance from London and London is where my ex-wife is."

Fleur blinked. Lord this guy was straightforward if nothing else. He'd caught her off guard by mentioning an ex-wife.

Patrick sipped his wine, staring at her over the rim of his glass. "I'm sorry. I've made you feel uncomfortable, haven't I?"

"No, no you haven't, really." She bought time by tasting her drink. It was good, slightly fruity just how she liked it. He still watched her, waiting for a comment. She put her glass down. "Not many men would admit to hiding from an ex-wife. Information like that wouldn't normally be revealed for hours yet, and until a lot of alcohol had been drunk."

He laughed softly. "That's true, but I'm not your average guy." His eyes lit up in subtle meaning and she was lost on a wave of desire again. She was dreaming. She had to be. No one really had dates with drop-dead gorgeous guys. It was the stuff of fairy tales.

She played with the stem of her glass. "I take it your ex-wife wouldn't venture to Whitby?"

"No." He snorted and drank some of his wine. "My former wife likes the bright lights of a big city and, if she has my money to spend, she likes it even better."

Fleur sat back in her seat. *He's bitter.* She was saddened by the tight line of his sensual mouth as he spoke of his wife. She wanted to reach out and ease his hostility. Such an attractive man shouldn't carry his obvious resentment like a weight on his back. He represented a successful, sophisticated man, yet she had just glimpsed that not all was happy in his world, and it intrigued her. "Have you been in Whitby long?"

"Nearly three years. Before that I had a restaurant in London." He paused while Angela placed their entrée on the table and left. "My plan was to open a chain of restaurants up and down the country."

"It was a plan, but now it's not?"

He sighed and a frown appeared. "I'm not sure now. I lost my London restaurant in my divorce. Julie, my former wife, claimed she was entitled to half of it because she helped set it up. That was true, she did help with promotions, décor and stuff, but she put no money into the business. Anyway, I didn't have the stomach to fight her. Was only too happy to get the hell out of there."

"That's tough."

"Yes, well, in the end it was easier to close it down and give her a stack of money and say goodbye. My interest had waned for that particular restaurant because she was associated with it."

Fleur's soup went cold as she listened to him. He had a perfect voice for listening to, the Irish accent was there but not overpowering. It astounded her that he was so open, so frank with her when she was a complete stranger. "You shouldn't let that bad experience stop you from carrying out your plan to open more restaurants."

"No, I shouldn't, but..." he hesitated, "money was tight for a while."

Fleur blushed and lowered her lashes, hoping he didn't think her nosy. She couldn't believe he was giving her so much of him. Usually, men clammed up over their private lives and getting information out of them was like opening up a padlock without a key.

"Do you like the soup?"

She smiled and took a spoonful. "Yes, it's very delicious."

"So, now I've surprised you by speaking so openly, unlike most men, what about you?" He grinned and she relaxed again, liking his simpleness, his honesty. It was so refreshing.

"What would you like to know?"

Humor lurked beneath his direct gaze. "Favorite color."

"Blue."

"Favorite song."

"Um, anything by Robbie Williams. But then, I also like most types of music, except heavy rock. I love dancing." She sipped her wine and then Patrick refilled her glass and his own.

"Favorite movie."

She grinned. "This is a hard one. There's too many. Maybe *Steel Magnolias.*"

He chuckled. "I like that too."

"No." She stared at him wide-eyed. "A chick flick?"

He nodded. “I enjoyed the dry humor.”

“Me too.” She finished her soup and wiped her lips on a napkin.

“Dogs or cats.”

“Dogs.” She laughed, liking the game, though she realized they were drawing stares from the staff, especially Angela. Perhaps they weren’t used to seeing their boss enjoying a dinner with a female? She dismissed them from her mind and concentrated on Patrick. “And you?”

“Dogs. Though my mum has a very clever parrot that talks. Whenever they have a visitor walk through the door, he tells them to sit and take the weight off their feet.”

“An ice breaker.” Fleur giggled.

“Absolutely. Only my aunt, who is a rather large lady, takes it personally and my dad always adds his little comments to stir the pot.”

She laughed. “So, do you have brothers and sisters?”

The laughter in his eyes died and suddenly his wineglass became the focus of his attention. “I did. A sister. She died in a car accident.”

“I’m sorry to hear that.”

He sighed and looked at her. “Tell me about Australia. I’d like to go there.”

“Perhaps you could open a restaurant out there?” She gave him a sinful smile. “We have wicked St Patrick’s Days.”

He laughed and leaned forward to rest his elbows on the table. His eyes darkened, intensifying their blueness. “If all Aussie girls are like you, I just might.”

Chapter Three

"I still can't believe it, you know." Rachel shook her head and dipped her brush in the paint tin.

Fleur smiled and knew she blushed just thinking about Patrick, who had been the main topic of conversation since Rachel appeared this morning. "Why? Why is the knowledge of Patrick Donnelly and I having dinner together so hard to believe?"

Rachel stared at her. "Because he's gorgeous and because he's not had a girlfriend in all the time he's been here. Then you turn up and bang, he's inviting himself to your table."

"Well, I could hardly refuse him, could I? It was a free dinner after all." She placed her roller in the paint tray. "Anyway, how do you know he hasn't had a girlfriend since he's been here?"

"Gossip, how else?"

"From what I can gather his ex-wife burnt him pretty badly."

"She must have, because he hasn't sent out any signals to lure another. You don't have any idea how rare great-looking and successful guys are around this area." Sitting on her bottom, Rachel shuffled further along the floor to continue painting the skirting board. "Honestly, it's not really fair. You've only been here five minutes and you've taken the best guy around."

Fleur spluttered with laughter, holding onto the ladder for support. "I have *not* taken Patrick Donnelly off the single's market at all."

"Did he walk you home?"

"Yes, I told you he did."

"And?"

"And what?" Fleur took on an innocent expression. "You want to know if he kissed me?"

Rachel rolled her eyes. "Well, duh, yes!"

"No, he didn't kiss me." She sighed and shook her head at her own stupidity. "I botched it completely. I think he might have wanted to, but I chickened out and literarily ran inside."

"Why?"

"I don't know." Fleur sat on the ladder step. "No, that's a lie, I do know."

"You don't have to tell me. I'll shut up and just paint."

"It's okay, really." She dabbed her roller into the tray below, watching the paint coat the sponge. "I'm attracted to him."

"There's nothing wrong with that." Rachel dipped her brush again. "Aren't you looking for a guy?"

"I hadn't thought to, no." Fleur stood and rolled paint onto the ceiling. She hadn't realized how painting a ceiling could let her mind wander to things she had shied away from in recent years. Coming to England had been a reprieve from hospitals and doctors visits. Finding a lover had been last on her list, well, it hadn't actually even *made* her list.

Rachel scrambled up from the floor. "Shall I put the kettle on?"

Nodding, Fleur rested her roller against the wall and followed her into the kitchenette.

Wiping her hands on an old towel, she watched Rachel click on the kettle's switch and then put sugar and coffee into two cups. With no effort on either part, she and Rachel had formed a solid foundation to a friendship very easily. Though this surprised Fleur, she was also amazed at her need to talk to Rachel unlike no one else, not even her mum, who she was close to.

Fleur went to the tiny fridge, took out the bottle of milk and handed it to Rachel. "Eighteen months ago I had surgery for breast cancer."

Rachel spun around and stared at her. "Oh, Fleur. Christ, are you okay?"

"I am now."

"Are you cured?"

"They say so." She shrugged. "Who can ever tell?"

The kettle boiled and Rachel switched it off. "You are young to get it."

"I was twenty-seven when they told me."

They took their coffees into the shop and sat on the old cover sheets with a packet of biscuits between them.

"Is that why you aren't looking for a guy?" Rachel asked.

"Partly." Fleur sucked in a deep breath. "I had chemotherapy for months. My hair fell out and all that." She stared at the steam rising from the cup. "After being through such a demoralizing situation, you tend to think differently about everything."

"I can imagine."

"Before they found the cancer I was a bit of a party girl." She gave Rachel a wry grin. "I went backpacking for a few years.

Lived in different countries. Had some incredible times. I did so much that I wanted to do. I lived for the moment. The future was something a long way off. Then I got cancer and it all changed."

"You must have been so frightened."

"Yes, I was." She closed her eyes momentarily, thinking back to those dark days when she thought she'd never make it. "The day I finished my last chemo session, I instantly knew that partying every weekend and doing odd jobs to pay for my next overseas trip had to stop. Something inside me said I needed to change. I needed to focus on the future that I had suddenly been granted."

"What, like settle down?"

Fleur nodded. "Something like that. My mum and dad paid for me to have my eggs frozen before I started chemo."

"Wow." Rachel stared wide-eyed. "I've heard of it, but never known anyone who had it done. That's so generous of them."

"Yes, it is." Fleur sipped her coffee. "I told Mum and Dad that I wanted to go back to England for six months or a year. You see I've been here before. Mum and Dad are English and I came here with them once for a holiday. I always wanted to come back and live here to really get to know and understand my heritage. I've got extended family everywhere in this country. I felt that it was a part of me that I'd really like to explore. Do you know what I mean?"

Rachel nodded and selected a biscuit without looking, giving Fleur her whole attention. "But just because you've had cancer doesn't mean you can't have a boyfriend or get married or have kids, especially since you have eggs frozen."

"I know. That's my point. I never wanted to settle down until I found out I had cancer. Coming here was my last flight of total independence." Fleur rubbed her fingers across her forehead. “Meeting Patrick wasn’t meant to happen. I didn’t want a relationship until I returned home.”

“Well, I can understand that.”

“I’m not staying here forever. Just the summer or a year at the most. Then I want to go home, find a great guy and get married and maybe try and have kids.”

“And you don’t want to fall in love while in England.”

“Definitely not. It becomes too complicated.”

“Well, what are you going to do about Donnelly?”

“Stay away from him.”

Rachel took another biscuit. “That shouldn’t be so hard to do.”

“Let’s hope not.”

“Or you could have a wild, passionate affair with no strings attached,” she said innocently.

Fleur’s stomach flipped at the thought and she realized that anything remotely wild or passionate with Patrick was just what she wanted.

Fleur signed the deliveryman’s docket and, after he left, glanced around the shop. Towards the back, a stainless steel counter with a glass display stood at right angles with the wall. In the other corner was a glass door fridge, ready for cans of soft drink. They would be the only two modern pieces of furniture in the shop. She didn’t like the coldness of the steel but it was necessary for food.

Walking around behind the counter, her mind ran with plans. Her list was upstairs but she knew what still had to be bought. Tables and chairs, tablecloths, hundreds of books, crockery and cutlery—

"Hello." Patrick stood leaning against the shop's open front door. "You've been busy."

He wore jeans and a blue T-shirt and oozed sex appeal. Her response to him was automatic and deeper than she'd experienced with any other man before. He simply took her breath away.

"Hi, Patrick." She smiled and hoped color didn't flood her cheeks, as her heart skipped a thousand times faster than normal.

She hadn't seen him since dinner last week and as much as she had wanted to, she hadn't gone out of her way to contact him. The polite thank-you card she'd sent to the restaurant had been it. She had fought her tendency to constantly think about him, knowing it was for her own sanity. As she had told Rachel, staying away from him was the wisest thing to do. However, she didn't realize how hard that would be.

"You don't waste any time, do you?" He stepped further into the shop and looked around. "The paint color is a good choice. Lemon is sunny, cheery."

"I thought for summer it would be a good color and with the white ceiling, it contrasts nicely."

"What about furniture, table and chairs?"

"I've been told of a warehouse that sells old secondhand furniture, I thought to try them."

Knocking at the back door interrupted them. A large, hairy man, wearing baggy shorts and a shirt too small for him, wandered into the shop. "Hello there. I'm looking for Fleur Stanthorpe. We got a coffee machine for her."

"Yes, that's me. I wasn't expecting you until this afternoon."

"Where would you like it, luv?" He hitched his shorts up over his protruding stomach, drawing emphasis to his skinny white legs.

"On the end of the counter there." Fleur turned to grin at Patrick.

Patrick, hiding his laughter, walked with her into the kitchenette. "Is there anything I can do?"

From the bench she picked up a tape measure and pencil. "Could you help me measure the walls for the bookshelves? I need to order the timber."

"Sure." He smiled and took the tape measure from her.

Their hands touched and Fleur's gaze locked with his. Her smile froze as his eyes narrowed in a desire he didn't hide. Her heart thumped. *Has he been thinking about me during this last week?*

"Just through here, then, luv?" The deliveryman puffed, walking backwards with his end of the coffee machine.

"Yes, keep going." She waited until he and his partner had gone through into the shop before looking at Patrick again. "I don't want to hold you up if you're busy."

"I'm not busy. Well, I am, but it can wait." He winked and shivers of pleasure flooded her.

Fleur sniffed the delicious aroma of fish and chips smothered in vinegar. "I'm so hungry."

Patrick ate a chip straight from the paper wrapping and gazed around the improved shop. "We've worked hard."

Timber shelves lined two walls from floor to ceiling. A large, scalloped, white lace curtain hung from the front window and matching lace tablecloths covered the five tables.

"I can't thank you enough for all your help." She poured them both a soft drink and handed his glass over. "Without your assistance I wouldn't have accomplished so much in such a short time."

"You don't have to thank me, I enjoyed it."

"Despite having your own workload?"

"Donnelly's nearly runs itself. I have good staff."

"Yes, I know, but I feel guilty keeping you away from your new venture."

"I've told you that you haven't." He gave her a playful-scolding look. "Before anything happens with the new restaurant in Manchester, there's a heap of paperwork, planning approval and all the other red tape to sort through."

"I'm pleased you've thought to expand."

He took her hand and squeezed it softly. "It's with thanks to you. When we had dinner you made me realize that I was wallowing in self-pity and that's not very attractive, especially when I was desperate to impress you."

She stared at him open-mouthed. His honesty always surprised her. "Impress me?"

"Of course." Laughter came into his blue eyes. "I think I failed terribly."

She sucked in a deep breath. "You didn't fail at all."

"Good." He took another chip, but didn't let go of her hand and she wasn't in any hurry to break their contact.

For the last three days she had fought to behave properly in front of him and show no sign of her attraction. There were times when she wanted to do nothing more than throw her arms around him and beg him to kiss her until she couldn't breathe, but gathering all her willpower, she ignored her yearnings. At odd times she caught him looking at her and he would smile wryly, even a little sadly, though why she didn't know.

"When's opening day?"

Startled out of her thoughts, Fleur concentrated on tearing apart her piece of fish. "In two weeks. The weather is becoming warmer and I think people will start making daytrips now."

"Yes, June's weather is more reliable than May's."

"A local newspaper reporter and photographer are coming tomorrow to interview me and take some photos. It should feature in the Wednesday's newspaper just in time for opening day. But first I have to fill these shelves with books. I thought I might go to a few car boot sales this weekend and the next. I've also placed advertisements in the local newspaper for anyone wanting to get rid of books to drop them off here and I'll give them a few pounds for them."

"Car boot sales?"

She smiled at his doubtful expression. "Yes, they have great bargains."

"I could take you if you'd like?"

Her heart soared. "Thank you. I'd like that."

Chapter Four

Fleur handed over the money to the older woman on the other side of the table. She got such a buzz when buying bargains and this morning she had done exceptionally well.

She thanked the woman and picked up the three bags of secondhand books she'd just bought for only a few pounds. Around her the noise of a successful car boot sale filled the air. Children laughed and shrieked, having eaten too many sugary goodies. From somewhere a dog barked and a baby cried.

The slight breeze whipped Fleur's hair into her eyes as she looked around for Patrick. He'd returned to the car with his arms loaded with bags of books she had bought half an hour before and that was the last she'd seen him.

Her heart sang whenever she thought of him, which was nearly every minute of the day. How had she managed to capture the interest of this wonderful man?

For two weeks they had been inseparable. He had called each day to help set up the shop or to take her away for an hour, giving her a break from all the tasks opening a business required. She had cooked for him when the days ran late with decorating or assembling things for the shop. Other times, they had gone to the restaurant and had dinner. This, naturally, caused secretive looks between Patrick's staff but generally they were warm and friendly towards her. She couldn't stop them from gossiping and neither did she really care.

The best times though, were like today, driving through the countryside in his sleek car, listening to music—she had converted him into a Robbie Williams fan now and he'd surprised her by buying the singer's latest two cds.

The Saturday before had been the first car boot sale Patrick had attended, and Fleur couldn't help laughing at his wary expression as they'd pulled up in the car park. It had taken Patrick a lot of convincing that car boot sales and garage sales were the cheapest way for her to get the books to fill the shop. He'd spent the couple of hours it took her to go around the whole field staring in amazement at the stuff people displayed on tables and blankets on the ground.

This time, the sale was a larger gathering and within minutes of arriving she had lost Patrick as he swarmed over the tables and stalls looking at dvds, cds, leather belts, winter jackets and old model cars. He was like a kid in a sweets shop and she couldn't help laughing at him.

Now, though, it was getting late and spots of rain descended from heavy dark clouds. Deciding to head for the car, she saw Patrick emerge from behind a stall, licking a large ice cream; in his other hand he held one for her.

As she drew near, she grinned and raised her eyebrows. "Where have you been? I thought you were coming straight back?"

He licked his ice cream and winked. "I got sidetracked. I had other things on my mind."

"Like ice cream?" She gave him a saucy look, but her insides melted whenever he smiled at her. Together they turned for the car.

He held out her cone. “Ice cream is very important. You simply can’t go out for the day and not have one. It’s tradition.”

She laughed and held up the bags. “How can I eat it with this lot?”

“Oh dear. Looks like I’ll have to eat yours too then,” he joked, but just then a large raindrop splattered onto his ice cream and he frowned in surprise, which made Fleur giggle.

The rain fell heavier, and a clap of thunder rolled in the distance. People started to move quicker, heading for their cars as the only shelter, while the sellers hurriedly packed up their goods.

“I think we’d better run for it,” Patrick said, squinting into the windblown rain.

They ran through the rows of cars looking for Patrick’s navy BMW. On a hasty mission to get into the car without getting any more soaked than they already were, Patrick, juggling ice creams in one hand, opened the boot for Fleur to throw in the bags on top of the others. Hurrying, they jumped into the car and slammed the doors.

Fleur glanced at Patrick, dripping not only rain from his hair but also ice cream from the cones he held in each hand, and laughed. Despite his appearance she thought he looked damn fine. Sexy as hell.

A box of Kleenex sat between the seats and she grabbed a couple to wipe the dripping, sticky mess.

“Can you wipe my eyes first?” He chuckled. “I can’t see properly.”

Leaning over, she gently wiped his wet face. Her movements were long and leisurely. She liked having the opportunity to touch him in all innocence. Yet, when she caught his gaze, his eyes were dark with unspoken messages and the pit of her stomach curled in anticipation. Innocent, her backside. Wicked thoughts plagued her.

Slowly he bent forward and touched his lips to hers. Her breathing seemed suspended between her lungs and throat. Her hand holding the Kleenex fell to his shoulder as she leaned in closer, wanting so much more than he was giving her at the moment.

Their kiss deepened, intensified. His tongue stroked hers in a slow dance, tasting, exploring. An ache spread from the very core of her to reach from the top of her head to her toes. Heat flamed her body.

"I've wanted to kiss you since the first day I saw you," he murmured.

"Me too..." She drew back a little and smiled shyly.

"I haven't fancied anyone for a long time, you know that?" Patrick leaned forward and kissed her nose, then her eyes. "Then you came along and the instant I saw you I was lost for words."

"Really?" Wide-eyed, she stared at him. "It didn't seem that way."

A wry smile lifted the corners of his mouth. "Do you think I just invite anyone for a free meal at my restaurant? I had to get to know you."

"I'm so glad you did."

"Mmm... I am too."

She pressed herself against his chest. That he still held the cones and couldn't touch her with anything but his mouth made it so erotic.

As if reading her mind, he brought his cone in between them.

Together they licked the melting ice cream and then kissed, sometimes transferring the confectionary into each other's mouths. Fleur used her finger to dip into the ice cream and traced around his lips with it. The tip of her tongue followed the pattern she made and Patrick groaned deep in his chest.

In seconds he had opened the door, thrown both cones out and slammed the door shut again.

As the rain beat hard against the windscreen, he dragged her over the seat divide and onto his lap. Holding her tight, he kissed her with mounting passion until she could barely breathe. He created a blaze of fire within her and she felt she would self-combust if he didn't quench the ache soon.

Fleur squirmed on his lap, feeling his erection and wanting it inside her, wanting him to bring her to the peak and then allow her to fall delicately back down. It had been so long since a man needed her, desired her, and she'd missed that.

A sharp tapping on the window startled them both and guiltily they sprang apart.

Patrick wiped the foggy window to clear it and an old man peered in at them.

"Listen, you two." The old fellow's eyes narrowed in anger and he tapped against the window again even though he had their full attention. "I'll not have that sort of behavior here, thank you very much! There are young kiddies about. Now get off home. You should know better at your age."

Feeling as in the wrong as when her father had caught her coming in home late at night when she was a teenager, Fleur sidled back over to her seat and reached for her seat belt. Her cheeks flamed with embarrassment.

Patrick fired the engine into life and reached for his seat belt too. His eyes held humor and Fleur bit her lip to hide her grin. She felt so alive.

Maneuvering the car out of the field, Patrick chuckled. "It's been a long time since I was told off for making out in my car."

Fleur laughed and settled back as Robbie Williams sang to her from the speakers, and tried to ignore the throbbing of her unsated body. Every movement Patrick made had her body responding inwardly, yearning for his touch.

The heavy rain accompanied them all the way home and they grew quiet as Patrick concentrated on the grey, misty weather. However, it was an easy silence between them, no awkwardness, and for that Fleur was eternally grateful.

In the yard behind the shop, Patrick parked the car, and they unloaded the boot before going inside.

Fleur dumped the bags of books in the kitchenette and turned to speak to Patrick, but before she could utter a word, he pulled her into his arms.

"You drive me crazy, woman. Do you know that?" he whispered, his voice husky.

His lips softly traced the outline of her mouth. Delicately, he kissed her bottom lip, then her top lip, before gently nibbling her bottom lip again, prolonging the full invasion of her mouth. Patrick's hand hugged the curve of her waist, then preceded down to grip her hips and pull her even closer against him.

An aching of want spiraled in the center of her being. She ran her hands up to the back of his head and threaded her fingers through his damp hair. Flicking her tongue out, she tasted him. His tongue caressed hers, teasing her, building within her a hunger that only he could satisfy.

Fleur inched her hands around his waist and down to his backside.

"I want to make love to you," he said, his mouth hot against hers. He gathered her close, arching her into his body. His teeth lightly nibbled her earlobe, sending shivers of delight down to the pit of her stomach. "Is it too soon?"

She blinked, trying to think, and ignored the flame of wanting he had built into an inferno inside her. "I...I don't know, is it?"

His soft chuckle filtered through her uncertainty and she stared at him as he pulled away slightly. "Two, no, three weeks. Not exactly a one-night stand, is it?"

"No." But was it long enough to take it the step further? She didn't know the yardstick to measure such questions by. She couldn't think when in his arms.

Patrick kissed her again, long and slow.

Trembling faintly, wanting him so much, she rubbed her hips against his.

His hand found her breast and his thumb circled her nipple.

She instantly stiffened. He'd touched the breast that had been treated for cancer. He was the first man to do so who wasn't a doctor.

He raised his head to look at her. "What's the matter?"

"Nothing. Sorry." Her smile was strained she knew, but she couldn't help it. It wasn't as if she didn't want him to touch, she did. Her breast didn't hurt and the scar was very small. Yet, she had long stopped thinking about her breasts as something sensual or alluring. They had been probed and prodded by medical professionals for so long now that the thought of someone actually finding them sexual turned her stomach, the knowledge of which she had just found out for the first time.

"It is too soon?"

"What?" She blinked, and then blushed, knowing she had forgotten his presence with her worries. "I'm sorry, Patrick."

He pulled away, stepping out of her arms. “It’s fine, really. My fault completely. I tend to rush when I want something.”

The break in physical contact made her feel alone, bereft. She hugged herself and glanced away. Lord, what a mess. If she behaved like this every time a man touched her breast she’d never have sex again. Or a partner. But then, she didn’t want just anyone, she wanted Patrick—only Patrick—and that sudden admission startled her.

“I’d best go.” Patrick lingered, and then, as if making up his mind, he strode to the door and opened it. The look he gave her was soft and tender. “Ring me?”

“Yes, I will.”

“Promise?”

“Of course.” Through the window, Fleur watched him walk to the car and climb in, within seconds he was driving away up the street.

Sucking in a deep breath, she plodded upstairs and flopped down on the sofa. She wrinkled her nose, deflated. Her body ached as though she’d run a mile. Obviously, being left unsatisfied wasn’t healthy. Good sex left you on a high and if you were tired it meant you had a good workout, too. But this strung-up feeling did nothing for a natural high. In fact, it was the opposite.

Did she really want to go on this ride—this roller coaster of emotions, wants and needs?

Rachel’s words rang in her mind. *A wild and passionate affair.* Well, that wasn’t going to happen no matter how much she wanted to. Why start something she knew would end with her tears? An affair sounded fun and exciting, but at the end, when it was time to go home to Australia, would she be able to walk away from a smart, sexy man such as Patrick?

The answer was a resounding no.

There'd be tears and hurt and she'd had enough of that in the last couple of years to last a lifetime. Fleur sighed and sagged against the cushions.

She wasn't going to phone him. Definitely not. She hadn't actually said the word "promise", had she? So she wasn't going back on her word then, was she?

Damn!

Already he'd gotten her twisted into knots.

No. It was best all around if they stayed away from each other. She was here for only a short time to spend an English summer selling books and coffees. That was her plan and it was a good one. Preparing for this adventure had saved her sanity while undergoing chemotherapy and no good-looking Irishman was going to ruin it.

Fleur wiped the counter with a damp cloth and glanced around the shop. Muted talk filled the room, nearly drowning out the low hum of the local radio station playing from the stereo she'd set up in the kitchenette.

Rachel stood by the tables nearest to the window, talking to friends who had come in for a coffee and to check out the newest shop in town.

Fleur hadn't the faintest idea what she'd have done in the last month without her neighbor. Rachel was one of those amazing people who was instantly friendly and helpful and who made you wonder how you ever lived without them before.

They'd become firm friends with Rachel working in the shop without complaint. Fleur had given her a small wage in cash, so it didn't disrupt her benefits, and even though Rachel had refused the money at first, Fleur had insisted, knowing that as a single mother, Rachel would need all the help she could get. Besides, she had worked for it. The only regret Fleur had was that she couldn't afford to give her full-time employment, but as successful as the business was, it would never make enough for two wages and expenses.

The shop had been open for two weeks. Two busy, exhausting, frantic weeks when she'd hardly had time to draw breath. So far it had been an outstanding success.

Opening day had been the Saturday before last. She'd organized the local press to be there when she opened the door at eight-thirty. The smell of fresh coffee and delicate pastries had encouraged passersby to come in and have a look.

For the first hour it was all free. Each customer was given a coffee, a pastry and a secondhand book. She and Rachel worked nonstop until nearly one o'clock. A good deal of the time was spent talking to the local people explaining what she was offering—a place to come and relax.

As the days rolled into the end of June and the weather became warmer and tourists became more in quantity, she had found a few customers were returning. Some came only to buy the cheap books, others came only for the coffee and cakes, but what pleased her most was the odd regular who came wanting to sit in a spot of sunshine by the window and sip their coffee and browse the newspaper or flip through a book. She had created a little bit of heaven right here in Whitby for those needing an hour of relative peace or a break from their everyday life.

She had opened the shop everyday, with longer hours on the weekends, when the tourist numbers were at their height. Yet, despite working fourteen days straight, she was not weary of it. Indeed, keeping busy was the only thing that helped to stop her mind from straying into the murky waters of her friendship with Patrick.

Patrick.

He had arrived on the shop's opening morning and remained silent and unobtrusive in the corner, holding a coffee in his hand as she mingled with the people flowing in and out.

She had fought a battle to stop her gaze from straying towards him all the time. He was like a magnet, constantly pulling at her, drawing her attention, her thoughts. When she caught him staring at her, she'd lost her train of thought and had to ask the customer to repeat their order.

Such gut-wrenching magnetism fascinated and worried her. She didn't want the distraction, certainly didn't need it or Patrick in her life, but what could she do about it?

Before leaving the shop, he had taken her hand, kissed her cheek and wished her well. He also told her he was going to Manchester for a week.

She hadn't seen him since.

Two whole weeks.

Had he dropped her like a hot potato?

Was one rebuff enough to send him away never to return?

Her reaction to him touching her breast had been simply instinctive. No harm in that surely? Obviously it wouldn't happen again. She was prepared now. Still, an affair with him was out of the question.

She might not have seen him and she might not have wanted to think about him, but the truth was he played on her mind a lot. Too much.

Alone in her bed, she recalled their kisses, her body burning for his touch. His sexy smile that darkened the blueness of his eyes would flash before her, making her squirm in the sheets, longing for him. It was like he'd branded her with his imprint, only his touch could satisfy, and without it, she was left stranded like a boat with no rudder. She didn't like that feeling, that dependence.

"Could I have a black coffee, please?"

Fleur blinked, and abruptly realized she had mentally shut out the shop and her customers. Heat burnt her cheeks. "I am so sorry. I was miles away. Good lord how embarrassing, please forgive me."

The woman opened her purse, smiling all the time, as she took out the required coins. "Yes, of course. It's perfectly okay. I do it all the time. Especially when my husband is watching the football."

Fleur smiled, quickly making the coffee. "Is there anything else you wanted?"

"Well, I fancy a piece of that lovely banana cake there, but my hips won't thank me for it."

Sliding the cup and saucer across the counter with one hand, Fleur bent and took a small plate from the shelf underneath. "How about one tiny slice on the house, just for you to taste. Your hips wouldn't begrudge you that I'm sure. Call it a taste experiment." She grinned. "Take a seat and I'll bring it over."

She took the cake stand from out of the display and deftly cut a thin piece of cake. She arranged it on the plate and next to it squeezed a flower-shaped dollop of fresh cream. On top of that she added a large strawberry, split in half and dipped in chocolate. She suddenly heard her Uncle Harry's words—"spoil them and they'll keep coming back for more". Good ole Uncle Harry.

"There goes my diet." The woman beamed when Fleur placed the plate in front of her.

"The best diet in the world is the one that includes a little bit of everything." Fleur winked. Moving away, she glanced out of the window. Angela, Patrick's waitress, stood outside staring back at her. Fleur lifted a hand to wave, but Angela turned her back on her. Startled, Fleur frowned. The other woman's expression hadn't been friendly.

With a shrug, Fleur wiped down a few tables. She had suspicions that Angela was half in love with Patrick. Yet, he had given Fleur no indication that he felt anything in return or that they might have had a past relationship. Would Patrick have done something like that? Had an affair with his waitress? The mere thought made her feel sick. She didn't even want to accept the concept of Patrick touching another woman, never mind making love to someone else...

She spun around to go back to the counter but stopped abruptly on seeing Patrick enter the shop. Her heart seemed to fall to the bottom of her stomach and bounce back up again to lodge in her throat. She stared, drinking in the sight of him, replenishing her mind and senses of his every feature. It had been too long, way too long since she last saw him.

Why hadn't he called before now? He must have been home at least a week.

He wasn't wearing his glasses, and crazily she thought they must be for when he was reading only. She was rather disappointed he wasn't wearing them, as she thought he looked sexy with them on. Her gaze raked over him, noting his black trousers, his grey shirt, black tie. Sex. He was a living advertisement for sex—and of what a man in his prime should be. Hard, lean, attractive, assured. She wanted him so badly.

"How are you, Fleur?" His accent caressed her, made her insides melt. Did her legs actually wobble? It felt like it. She felt unstable from top to toe and all he did was speak to her.

She took a step towards him, but Rachel tapped her arm, wanting her attention. Startled, Fleur frowned at her, slowly focusing on what she was saying. "Um, yes?"

Rachel, eyes wide in her face, leaned close to whisper, "I can handle the shop. Why don't you take Patrick upstairs to the flat before you actually drool right here in front of everyone?"

Oh my God.

Fleur closed her eyes momentarily, horrified at having been caught out staring at Patrick like a sex-starved nymphomaniac. Nodding like someone struck dumb, Fleur turned a tentative smile on Patrick. His slow grin made her die all over again. "W...Would you like to come upstairs?"

"Sure."

Climbing the stairs, Fleur hoped the flat was tidy. She did all the cooking in the small kitchen and was pedantic about cleanliness, but she wasn't sure she'd left the sitting room tidy. Long hours in the last fortnight had made her fall behind with the general housework. She hoped to God she didn't have knickers and bras drying on the stand near the window.

She gave the room a quick glance, relieved it was rather okay. Shoes littered one corner and a magazine still unread lay on the sofa. Oh, what the hell. He wasn't here to study her housework skills. Shyly smiling at Patrick, she went into the kitchen and opened the tiny fridge. Its startling bareness made her swallow back a rather bad swear word. Why couldn't she, just for once, be a hostess with the mostest?

"Would you like a drink? Something cold or a cup of tea?" She silently prayed he'd take a cup of tea. She had milk, but not much more. Grocery shopping suddenly became a high priority.

He shook his head, his gaze piercing her, rooting her to the spot.

"How have you been?"

"Good." Closing the fridge she stepped out of the kitchen and folded her arms. He was tense and so was she. Yuck. She smiled over-brightly. "And you?"

"Busy."

Obviously.

She feigned interest. "How was Manchester?" *Why didn't you contact me?*

"Hectic. I also made a rushed trip to Ireland to see my family. That's why I've been gone for longer than I expected."

"Oh, I see." Relief flooded her. He hadn't stayed away on purpose. Or had he?

Anyway, what the hell did it matter? She couldn't become involved with him.

This is awful.

They stood yards apart and seemed even more apart mentally. She liked having him as a friend, but the break hadn't done them any favors. Fleur sighed, wondering what he was thinking, and wondering what she could do to alter his serious expression.

The old, carefree, Fleur—the Fleur who once danced the samba in Rio on a hot summer's night with a Latin stranger—would have stormed straight up to him and kissed him soundly until he laughed. Only, she was older now, perhaps wiser, perhaps not, but a lot more cautious. Why or when she changed, she didn't know. It was like the brush with death was a wake-up call. The call to grow up and be responsible—that the time to be footloose and fancy-free was over. More importantly, she knew that Patrick wasn't someone who she could just pick up and leave as it suited her, and what's more, she didn't want to have him that way.

Patrick turned away and gazed out the window. “How long are you staying here for?”

The question surprised her. He had an amazing ability to just ask what was on his mind. She cleared her throat. For some reason she wanted the answer to be carefully thought out. Whereas before when Rachel had asked the same questions, she had shrugged and said a year maybe or just the summer, but now, with Patrick, she couldn’t find the words. “I’m not sure. It depends...”

He turned back to her, his expression unreadable. “Depends on what?”

She looked away and sat on the sofa. A cardigan had been thrown over the arm and she picked it up and folded it. “It depends on a lot of things.”

He nodded and gave her a quick smile that didn’t reach his eyes. “I have to go. I called in here first before going to my flat or to the restaurant. No doubt, I’ve got a heap of paperwork waiting for me and I’ve to check on the restaurant before we open for tonight’s trade.”

“Yes, of course.” She didn’t stand, didn’t trust her legs. Something had happened between them, he’d withdrawn from her and the loss hurt. She didn’t want him to leave, but it could be for the best. He had clearly been thinking about the future and whether his future included her, which it wouldn’t. They lived on either side of the planet.

Patrick pulled his car keys out of his pocket. “What time do you close tonight?”

“Around seven o’clock. The tourists stay out later now the nights are keeping lighter.”

“Long hours for you then.”

“Yes, but that’s okay. Sundays have proven to be one of my busiest days, it pays to stay open...” Her voice drifted off, she had the unexpected urge to cry. Why were they behaving like this? It was worse than when they first met. They had shared a few glorious weeks, enjoyed each other's company and kissed so passionately. Where had that closeness gone? Ignoring her sensible side, she wanted it back. She wanted it all back as to how it was before he went away.

He took a step, hesitated, and then smiled. "Are you open tomorrow?"

"Well, I was thinking of opening later in the day so I can catch up on some chores."

"Would you like to go out to lunch?"

Her heart thudded. She should say no. Spending more time together wouldn't help ease her from thinking about him constantly. However, she very much wanted to be with him. "I would like that. I'd have to speak to Rachel and ask her to mind the shop. I'm sure she will."

"I'll pick you up at twelve o'clock?"

"Yes, lovely. Thanks."

Patrick gave her a long lingering look, then quickly left the room and descended the stairs.

He exited the shop with only a glance in Rachel's direction and got into his car.

Leaning back against the seat, he paused before starting the engine. He hated being on edge, yet that's how he felt in Fleur's flat. The tension between them had sprung up after two weeks apart and it made him wonder if there was some hidden meaning to it all. Was he wasting his time? The promise of something wonderful between them had vanished.

He'd been an idiot not to phone her. But she had promised she would phone him and she didn't.

So he hadn't either.

He shook his head at his own stubbornness. Fool.

She had looked at him when he first walked into the shop as though she had missed him, but once in her flat she had been awkward and unsure.

Did she want to be with him? Was she regretting their brief involvement?

He sighed and wiped his hand over his tired eyes. Had he come on too strong? Perhaps he should rethink his intentions. She was here for only a short time. Maybe she only wanted a summer romance?

An affair?

He frowned in thought. He could *do* an affair. Of course he could.

Too easy.

Wasn't it every man's fantasy? He nodded slightly. A few months of good company...hot sex... Oh yes, he knew with a strange kind of certainty that making love with Fleur would be rather spectacular.

Patrick squirmed in his seat. An ache gripped his loins. It had been ages since he'd last slept with someone. A year ago there'd been a woman he'd met at a party back home and they'd spent an *entertaining* weekend together, but had, quite happily, gone their separate ways come the Monday morning. Since then all his energies and commitment had been ploughed into his business.

Was it enough?

Sadly, he realized it wasn't. Fleur Stanthorpe had opened his eyes to what he was missing. Company. Someone to laugh with, share things with, talk with and to make love with... He swore fluently and fired the engine to life. It would be ironic indeed if, for the first time, he truly opened his heart to a woman and it was rejected. He had an inkling that Fleur had the power to hurt him much more than Julie ever could.

Just my luck.

Chapter Five

The moment Patrick pulled in at the curb, Fleur left the shop and locked the door. He climbed out and came around to her side of the car, and with a cheeky grin opened the passenger door with an elegant bow. “Your chariot awaits, my fair maiden.” He winked.

Her stomach clenched in acute awareness of him. He wore casual clothes, cargo pants, a black T-shirt and expensive sunglasses. At once, the atmosphere between them was light and cheerful and Fleur sighed in relief. She’d hated the tension of his visit yesterday.

Taking the cue from him, she tilted her nose in the air and spoke with a posh accent. “Why, thank you, my good man.”

She settled into the seat and waited for him to jump in and start the engine. She tugged down the edges of her white shorts, hoping they weren’t too short or too tight. Perhaps she should have worn a flowing skirt or jeans? Groaning under her breath, she realized she’d missed shaving a spot near her knee. Typical. Fortunately, she still had her tan and it hid it well. Being an Aussie had its benefits.

“Did Rachel agree to run the shop?”

“Yes, but only for half the day because she had other commitments. She’ll open up in half an hour.”

“You okay with that?”

"Absolutely." She nodded and slipped on her sunglasses. "So, where are we going?"

Reaching for his seatbelt, he indicated to the backseat. A large wicker hamper and a red-checked blanket caught her eye.

"A picnic?" She smiled. He even did it properly with a blanket and basket. So traditional. She loved it. "Exquisite."

"The weather looks promising. How about we drive until we want to stop?"

"Excellent idea."

He pulled out into the lane. "Or I could take you sightseeing. We could go to York or Harrogate and look at the shops and stuff."

"You know what I'd really like?"

His glanced at her and flashed a sexy grin. "I'm all ears."

She laughed and playfully tapped his arm. "I'd like to go where there are no crowds and no town noise. I've seen people every day for the last couple of weeks and although that's good for business, today I'd like it to be just you and me. Is that okay?"

Patrick was silent for a moment before taking his hand off the steering wheel. He reached over and clasped her fingertips. He brought them to his mouth and kissed them, all the while his gaze never left the road in front. "You and me alone sounds great."

Tingles of sensual pleasure leapt up her arm from his gentle caress on her fingers. She yearned to lean over and kiss him fully. "Patrick?"

"Mmm?"

"We're going to have a great day."

"Yes, we are. I promise." He winked.

The radio played hits from the eighties and she turned up the volume to sing loudly and off-key.

They drove for an hour through the North York Moors with Patrick holding her hand. The blue sky and hot sun saturated the countryside. With the windows down, Fleur sniffed the fragrance of the summer wildflowers, and fully relaxed, gazed at the passing farm animals. She and Patrick talked a little, mainly about the things they passed and childhood memories, but generally they enjoyed the comfortable mood and felt no need to chat away endlessly.

"Hey, beautiful?"

Fleur turned her head from looking out at the passing moors to smile at Patrick. "You speaking to me?"

"I see no one else in the car, silly." He squeezed her hand. "It's after one and I'm getting peckish. Want to stop?"

"Well, I can hardly say no if you're hungry." She grinned. "We could perhaps have our picnic in a field. Do you think the farmer would be annoyed?"

He shrugged and shook his head. "No, I don't think so. How about over there?" Slowing down, he steered the car onto the roadside and parked beside a stone wall.

"Can traffic pass the car here?"

"Yep." Patrick nodded.

While he retrieved the hamper and blanket, Fleur climbed out of the car and walked to the wall. They were up high on moors. A blanket of purple heather and dried bracken stretched for as far as she could see broken only by the odd grey stone farmhouse and flocks of sheep in the distance.

"It's wonderful. I should have brought a camera," Fleur said as Patrick joined her.

"I've got one in the hamper." He grinned. "You don't think I'd have a day out with a gorgeous woman and not have the proof to show anyone, would you?"

She laughed. "Just another notch on your bedpost, am I?"

He leaned in close, his eyes alive with passion. "Are you offering?"

Intoxicated with life and excitement, Fleur leaned in even closer until she barely touched his lips with hers. "I might be..."

Patrick groaned. "Lord, woman, don't say such things when I have my hands full."

Fleur chuckled and, thankful that she wore shorts, climbed over the wall. "You'd better feed me, my good man," she called back as she sauntered away. "I have an enormous appetite."

They spread the blanket, flattening out the lumps and bumps beneath which released the scent of crushed heather. Patrick unpacked the hamper and Fleur raised her eyebrows in surprise at the amount of food he brought. Chicken, bread rolls, salad, cheese, crackers, strawberries and peaches.

She laughed, inspecting the bottle of wine and fizzy drink nestled amongst all the tasty fare. "It sure beats my attempts of throwing together some boiled egg sandwiches and a bottle of pop."

"I'm trying to impress here." He laughed. "Be appreciative."

"Oh, I am." She winked and nibbled on a strawberry.

"Good. Try some of this cheese." He forked a small piece onto a cracker and placed it in her mouth.

"Thank you," she mumbled, her mouth full.

Patrick held the camera to his eye. "Smile."

Fleur swallowed and posed so he could take the picture. She looked at the food. "I know I eat a lot, but that's more than even I can eat."

He cocked his head to one side, a wry grin playing about his lips. “There’s always the chance we’ll build up a large hunger.”

Chuckling, Fleur lay on the blanket, enjoying the warmth on her face. Her mother would be horrified that she wore no hat or sun protection cream. For a moment, the image of her mother’s face flashed before her. Their goodbyes at Sydney airport had been harder than ever. The closeness between them now had never been as strong. Cancer had done that. At least it had been good for something.

“Here you are.” Patrick handed her a tall flute glass of white wine and took another photograph of her.

“Oh, you thought of everything.” She took a sip. “It’s fruity just how I like it.”

“I know.” He smiled and poured himself a glass of Tango.

“You’re not having any?”

Shaking his head, Patrick stretched out alongside of her. “I never, ever, drink and drive.”

Fleur groaned inwardly. *No doubt he thinks I drink and drive all the time now.*

She wanted the ground to open up and swallow her whole. “Of course I didn’t mean that you do drink and drive...”

He glanced down at the fizzing orange drink in his hand. “A drunk driver killed my sister.”

“Oh, Patrick. I’m sorry, I didn’t realize.” She couldn’t meet his eyes and felt the warmth leave her face. “It must have been dreadful for you. I’m so sorry.”

“You weren’t to know. It’s okay.” He glanced up and smiled. “Today we can’t think of sad things or anything that will make us feel awkward. Agreed?”

"Yes. Good idea." She looked out over the rolling moors and into the hazy remoteness. "We were awkward yesterday in my flat. I hated that."

"Me too and I'm sorry. It was a bad idea to disappear for two weeks. Did you feel I'd forgotten about you? Did I let you down?"

She gazed at him, liking him, knowing that she was falling in love with him. *I'm going to get hurt.* "You didn't let me down, but I missed you."

"You didn't phone me."

"No."

He nodded, the tone of his voice sending a hidden message. "I understand."

"Really?"

"Really." He shrugged one shoulder. "Neither of us were expecting this."

"No."

"Kiss me." Desire darkened his blue eyes to navy.

Over their glasses, she leaned forward and lightly brushed her lips against his, savoring the feel of him. The lingering sweet taste of orange on his lips made it a little erotic. His wood scent cologne hung about him and she wanted to bury her head against his neck and stay there forever. So much for good intentions and all that...

"You call that a kiss?" he mocked.

"I haven't even begun," Fleur whispered, poking her tongue out to flick against his lips.

Patrick took her glass and placed it with his by the hamper, then encircled her waist with his hands and brought her against his chest. "Hold on tight, sweetheart, this could get messy," he breathed against her mouth.

She laughed and welcomed his kiss like someone starved. Heat curled in the pit of her stomach and as his tongue stroked inside her mouth the warmth spread out along her limbs. Arching into him, their legs entwined. From head to toe their bodies touched.

When Patrick's fingertips caressed her breast, she stilled but didn't draw away. Something in the back of her mind recognized the touch, but just at the same moment Patrick whispered how beautiful she was, and all self-doubt fled. She had done it. Thank God. She had got past the touching-the-whole-breast issue.

His hand moved lower onto her tummy and around underneath her to grasp her bottom and bring her hard up against him.

Grinning, she fully relaxed and tilted her head, giving him access to her throat. Shivers of delight tickled her skin as he nibbled her neck and shoulder. Clothes became a restriction. He ran his hand up and down her thigh, inching more under her shorts hem each time. His touch scorched her skin.

His breath grew short as Fleur traced the outline of his nipples through his shirt. Encouraged, she tugged up his shirt and pressed her hands on his hard, flat stomach. Touching his abdomen muscles, she hesitated. "No, it can't be."

Hitching up onto her elbow, she pushed him over onto his back, exposing his stomach, and stared. "Oh, I can't believe it."

"What?"

"You have a six-pack." Fleur laughed in amazement. "I've never gone out with a guy who actually had a six-pack before. This is brilliant." She ran her hands over the ridges his tight muscles made. "I think this is the best one I've seen, too."

Patrick looked amused. A lazy smiled played about his mouth. "A six-pack?"

"You know, a washboard stomach. They call it a six-pack at home." She pinned him with a steely gaze full of wickedness and her fingers walked across his satin skin. "You work out."

He nodded and lay back down with a grin. "I own a restaurant. If I didn't work out I'd be the size of a house. And I like the feeling of well-being after a good workout. Not as good as sex of course, but good nevertheless."

"This is so cool. I can't wait to tell my friends back home." Fleur, high on passion and excitement, bent down and kissed his toned body. Using the tip of her tongue, she circled his small bellybutton.

Patrick's intake of breath spurred her on and, as she continued to gently run her tongue over the taut flesh, her fingers inched his shirt higher. She teased his nipples with her tongue before drawing the bud softly between her teeth. She let the fingers of one hand glide down to the top of his waistband, teasing the flesh beneath.

"God, woman." He rolled them both over until she was under him, and he began to work his own brand of magic. His kisses grew hot and demanding and she loved it.

Hesitating a moment, he cupped her cheek with his free hand while the other hugged her to him. "I think we have a problem."

"Oh?"

"I want to make love to you right here on this blanket."

Fleur took a deep breath. She wanted it too. Lord how she wanted it. It wasn't wise. It would end in heartbreak, but she wanted this gorgeous man inside her, filling her, claiming her. He wanted her and without false modesty she knew he needed her beyond physical contact, too. It was that thought that terrified her the most.

He paused in kissing her neck. “Do you want to take the next step?”

“I don’t know…” She frowned, worried. “Yes, I do. I want to make love with you.”

Patrick looked deep into her eyes. “But?”

But.

She suddenly sat up, reached for her wine and took a sip. “I didn’t come to England for a holiday romance. Truly it was the last thing I wanted.”

“What did you come for?”

“A break.” She sighed and decided to lay all her cards on the table. “I had breast cancer and it’s kind of made me a bit screwy about what I want. I came here to try and find out.”

His eyes widened. Concern replaced the desire.

“Sorry, I didn’t mean to blurt it out like that. I’ve spoilt the mood now, haven’t I? Sorry.”

“Fleur…”

Biting her lip, she gave him a half smile. “I thought you should know. Why? I have no idea, but I suddenly had to tell you. Sorry. You said no unhappy talk.”

“Bugger that.” He sat up. “Come here and stop saying sorry.” He gathered her into his arms and kissed the top of her head. “I’m glad you told me. It means a lot to me that already you are trusting me. I’d like to know more if you want to speak of it. If not, then that’s okay, too.”

“I can talk of it. Actually I don’t mind talking about what happened because it’s something I can’t ignore all the time. There are days when I don’t think of it, but sometimes it haunts me and I long to speak to someone just to reaffirm that it’s gone and I’m healthy again.”

“Your family was there for you though?”

"Oh yes, definitely. They were brilliant. Very supportive. Only, I'm frightened of mentioning the cancer too much because it worries them and they've been through enough. Mum and Dad became really protective, which is natural I suppose. You never stop being their baby no matter how old you are."

Patrick kissed her gently, almost reverently. "Whenever you want to talk about it, night or day, then consider me as your first contact."

"Thank you."

"It must have been awful for you." His hold tightened.

"Yes, it was. I won't lie there. But I'm free of it at the moment. Had the surgery, chemotherapy and been given a clean bill of health. I still have to have regular checkups and everything, but it's in the past, at least for now. So, I'm going to be positive and enjoy England." She shrugged and nestled in closer. Being in his arms was paradise.

They were content to stay that way for a while and just listen to the quietness around them. The craziness of minutes before cooled but was still cloaking them with a special closeness. It all felt completely right. As it should be.

Patrick cleared his throat and shifted his weight a little. "What do you want to happen between us?"

Her stomach clenched at his bluntness. Sometimes his honesty was too honest. Fleur pulled away a bit to look up at his face. Had her cancer scared him off? Some men hated sickness of any kind and preferred not to get involved. "What do you mean?"

"Well, you're only in England a short time and...and we're enjoying each other's company, but I don't know the rules, Fleur." He frowned as if selecting the right words to say. "I don't know what to do."

"Neither do I."

"Is an affair enough or too much?" He sighed.

"I honestly don't know." She plucked a grass stem from beside the blanket. "I hate having to analyze this, but to let it happen naturally could mean we both get hurt."

"It might be too late for that anyway."

"I'm sorry, Patrick. I don't know the answers."

"Me neither. I thought I could do this. I thought an affair would be easy, fun. Only, I'm as scared as hell." He snorted in disgust. "Aren't I the cool one?"

"Do you want to stop seeing me?" Instinct made her tone sharp. She was already closing her heart towards possible pain. "I'd understand if you did."

He lowered his gaze to the blanket and glanced up at her from under his lashes. "No. I don't want to stop seeing you. I think you're great fun, beautiful and kind and very, very sexy, but I also don't want to be left brokenhearted."

Her bones melted. His tenderness and worry made her want to cry.

"Thank you for saying that and for being honest."

He nodded and put more distance between them. Building up his emotional walls, no doubt.

She reached up and ran her fingers through his dark hair. "Surviving cancer made me realize that I can't fling away my days and weeks on floating around the world on a whim."

"It sounds kind of good to me." He smiled sadly and, capturing her hand, kissed her palm.

"But I've been there and done it all. Patrick, I want a family, a home of my own. I'm nearly thirty years old and I have nothing to show for my life."

"So, after the summer you'll go home to Australia."

She nodded, unable to speak anymore. The heartbreak was already starting. The despair was already gathering speed, dragging her down. He stared down at her hand in his and played with her fingers. "What do you suggest we do? Have a good time together and then say goodbye in a few months or say goodbye today?"

A time frame? How can any relationship be defined by time? Perhaps this was the answer—have a great couple of months together and then go their separate ways. Did she want that though? One thing for sure was that she didn't want to think about it today, right now, this minute.

Fleur swallowed back her tears and tried to sound upbeat and cheerful. "Today is out of the question. I couldn't spoil all this food and sunshine. Let's just see what happens."

His blue eyes softened. "Yeah?"

"Yeah." She smiled and blinked away the heartbreak for now. Grabbing the camera, she took a photo of him. "Let's eat."

Patrick slowed down in front of the shop and turned off the engine. He looked at Fleur and need gripped his loins. "Did you have a good day?"

Fleur nodded. "The best."

He smiled and took a deep breath. His heart banged in his chest like a heavy metal drum player and he wondered fleetingly if it was the beginning of a heart attack. He'd had enough stress with Julie, he didn't think he could cope with another relationship going sour. But then, he'd always let his heart rule his head. "You know, I've been thinking."

"Dangerous." She grinned.

He raised an eyebrow at her sarcasm, and with a wry smile continued, "What are your thoughts about us just having a good time over the summer and then when it's time for you to go home, we'll reassess the situation. There is nothing that can't be worked out if we keep the lines of communication open."

She reached over and he met her halfway for a long, tender kiss that sent a tingle of sexual want right down to his toes.

"That sounds good to me."

"Sure?"

"Absolutely." Fleur nibbled his bottom lip and he groaned as pleasure circled his groin. He could barely think whenever he looked at her and how he'd not taken her on the blanket today he'd never know. It amazed him how much self-control he had. Still, it would be something special to look forward to once they did actually do it. And he planned on doing it all summer...

She sat back and smiled sadly. "I have to go. I've got much to do for tomorrow."

Sighing in disappointment, he nodded and, picking up her hand, kissed it. "I'm leading you astray."

"Yes, I know." She gave him another kiss and whispered, "I don't want to leave this car, but I have to. Sorry."

"That's okay." He ignored the hollow feeling at the thought of her leaving. "I have to go to the restaurant anyway. Can I ring you tomorrow?"

"You'd better do."

After another kiss, she slipped out of the car and ran lightly around to the curbside.

Patrick lowered his window and she leaned in to kiss him senseless once more. He watched her unlock the shop door and she waved from inside before disappearing out of sight. For a moment he sat there, blinded by the ache in his chest.

What have I done?

He'd fallen in love with someone who didn't even live permanently in this country. What kind of an idiot was he? He called himself all kinds of names.

"God, I'm a bloody fool." Patrick checked the mirrors for traffic and then drove up the narrow street. He thumped the steering wheel. "Get it together, Donnelly. You can do this. What man can't walk away after an affair? It's normal. It's expected, for Christ's sake."

Inside his head a small voice laughed, mocking him, telling him he wasn't the affair type of guy. How ridiculous. He wanted to deny it. Only, it was true. He didn't like affairs. They were too hard, too time-consuming and all you ended up with was nothing. For him it had to be all or nothing. Pathetic. He was letting down the male population across the whole world. There were standards to uphold for God's sake.

But, all jokes aside, he knew saying goodbye to Fleur Stanthorpe in a few months was going to be the hardest thing he'd ever do.

"I can't believe it." Rachel stood in the middle of the shop with a tray of glass pots full of sugar.

"Why can you never believe that Patrick and I spent time together?" Fleur tried to act hurt but instead laughed. "Don't you think I'm good enough for him?"

"Lord, no. It's not that at all." Rachel began distributing the sugar pots on each table. "You make a gorgeous couple, really. You're like something out of a magazine."

Fleur looked at her disbelievingly. "I doubt that very much."

"You fit each other well."

"Is there a 'but' here?"

"Well...it's just that he's known to keep himself to himself. It doesn't make sense that he's suddenly around town not caring if people see him with you." She gave Fleur a saucy look. "I guess that's what made him so appealing, his elusiveness, apart from his drop-dead good looks of course. No, you see, women like men of mystery." She nodded wisely and Fleur laughed even more.

"What rot." She shook her head, grinning, and continued to fill up the fridge with cans of soft drink. "Patrick isn't full of mystery. He's really very open. More honest than most men I've known."

"Aye, yes, to you maybe, but that's what makes it even more amazing because he's never gone out with someone in town before. Some even thought he was gay."

"Gay?" Fleur blurted out in a fit of laughter. The tiredness of being up since four a.m. cooking cakes and tarts disappeared.

Trying to look superior, Rachel sniffed. "All the gorgeous guys are gay. It's a known fact and a waste to the female population."

"I can tell you right now, he is not gay."

Rachel's eyes widened with anticipation of some juicy details. "Ooh la la. Do tell."

"As if."

"Spoilsport." Finished with that task, Rachel went behind the counter and started preparing the workspace for the day's trade.

Fleur looked at her. "So you believe he's never dated anyone from Whitby?"

Rachel nodded. "That's the general consensus."

"What about Angela the waitress at Donnelly's?"

"Angela Morrissey?" Tapping her finger against her lips, Rachel seemed to think hard about the question. "No. Definitely not."

"You seem sure."

"Well, there's no denying that Angela would jump at the chance to be Patrick's partner, but no, I don't think Patrick has even glanced her way, not in that sense anyway. If Angela ever had just a wink from Patrick in her direction, she'd let everyone know about it down at the pub. And as for a relationship, well, she'd have told *everyone*, believe me. She'd not have been able to help herself with him being such a good catch."

Fleur let out a breath she didn't know she'd been holding. Good. She trusted Rachel's opinion and now she wouldn't have to bring the subject up with Patrick.

Rachel folded her arms and a faraway look came into her eyes. "You know, I do envy you having such a lovely fella."

"You'll get one soon, I'm sure." Fleur pouted in sympathy and collapsed the empty cardboard box. "Isn't there a nice single dad at Courtney's school?"

"I wish."

"Hello there, ladies." A portly gentleman entered the shop. "I'm not too early for a cuppa, am I?"

"No, Mr. Hanley." Rachel smiled. "Sit yourself down and I'll bring you one over."

"Champion, lass." He sat by the window and with a nod to Fleur, opened his newspaper.

Smiling and feeling generally well pleased with her life at that moment, Fleur went out the back to place the box in the bin. The shop was earning a small profit, nothing grand, but enough to live off. The aim of the exercise wasn't to become a millionaire, simply to live among the English and get the feel of what her parents knew. She couldn't recapture the era they lived in, though she'd like to—the swinging sixties and all that. But she could understand them better when they reminisced about their lives in England.

Her mobile rang in her pocket, and thinking it was Patrick, was already smiling when she answered it.

"Fleur?" the voice in her ear yelled.

She paused by the back door. "Aunt Sal?"

"How are you, dear?"

"I'm fine, Aunt Sal. You don't have to yell. I can hear you just fine."

"I've never rung a mobile phone before. Do you want to come for lunch on Sunday?" she shouted.

Fleur held the phone away from her ear. "The shop is open all day Sunday. Sorry."

"I promised your mother I'd make sure you were eating properly."

"I am, Aunt Sal. Don't worry."

"You must come for your tea soon."

Grinning, Fleur could just imagine her aunt thinking she hadn't eaten a morsel of food since stepping out of her mother's front door. "Yes, I will, I promise. It's hard though with the shop being open six days a week, sometimes seven."

"Oh dear, I must go. Mrs. McCarthy across the way is out deadheading her flowers. Goodbye dear. Are you sleeping well?"

"Yes, I'm sleeping fine." Fleur chuckled.

"Goodbye then, dear."

"Bye, Aunt Sal."

The click was loud enough to be heard with the phone five inches from her ear. Fleur shook her head at the idiosyncrasies of her father's elderly aunt. Look out Mrs. McCarthy!

"Fleur," Rachel called from within the shop.

Tucking her phone into her jeans pocket, Fleur entered the shop and stopped in her tracks at the sight before her.

On every table was a large bunch of red and white roses tied with gold satin ribbon and above each bouquet, wafting delicately, were gold shiny balloons. The perfume of so many flowers nearly knocked her over. Fleur looked from the flowers to Rachel's surprised and excited face and back again. Her skin tingled with thrilling pinpoints of wonder and awe. Emotion blocked her throat as, wordlessly, she inched forward.

"By lass, that's a right set-up, that is." Mr Hanley stood at the counter in stunned amazement. "They just kept coming in and the van is still out the front now."

Fleur peeked between the flowers and balloons to see the florist step into the shop carrying a large spray of flowers that made Fleur's tears flow.

"Australian natives," she whispered to no one in particular. Reverently, she took them from the beaming florist and gazed through a misty veil of tears. Red waratahs, yellow kangaroo paws, pink grevilleas, dainty sprigs of white orchids and baby eucalyptus leaves.

Words would not form. She couldn't express her delight, her awe that someone would do this for her.

It must be Patrick.

Only he would have the class to do such a thing for her.

"Is there a card?" Rachel asked the florist.

"Yes, it's in the van." She hurried out and returned baring a bottle of wine with a white silk ribbon and a card attached.

"Heavens, Fleur. This is amazing." Rachel stared around the crowded shop. "I'd marry the guy who sent this to me."

For an instant Rachel's words bit deep. Marry Patrick? The thought startled her. She'd only known him five minutes, why did she even think such a thing? Heart thumping like she'd just run a mile, Fleur opened the card and read the sweet words.

Picnics will never be the same for me again.

Thank you for a perfect day.

Patrick.

An overwhelming feeling of love and affection filled her. "They are all from Patrick," she whispered to Rachel.

"As if we were in any doubt." She laughed.

Now it was confirmed, Fleur couldn't believe he would go to all that trouble and expense for her. He had made her feel special, cared for, wanted.

The florist left with Mr. Hanley following. Rachel picked up one basket of flowers and placed them on top of the counter. "They are so beautiful, but where are we to put them all?"

"I'll take most of them upstairs. You take a couple home, too."

Rachel's eyes widened. "Oh, I couldn't."

"Yes, you must." Fleur smiled. "Let's hope no one comes in who suffers from hay fever."

They took most of the displays upstairs and two went to Rachel's flat. The rest were placed around the shop, giving it a touch of freshness and class.

"I could get used to this." Rachel delicately touched one white rose of the nearest bouquet. "It's like something out of the movies."

Fleur nodded, still too stunned to speak coherently.

Two customers entered and Rachel went to serve them while Fleur remained gazing at the basket spray of the Australian natives. It was this arrangement more than anything else, which touched her deeply. This gesture had particular meaning. He acknowledged her connection with home.

"Rachel, I have to go see him to say thank you."

"Yes, go. I'll be fine."

"You sure?"

"Yes, just as long as you're back before three o'clock. I have to pick up Courtney from Mum's, as Mum goes to bingo tonight."

Fleur edged towards the door. "I'll be ten minutes tops."

"Nonsense." Rachel took the wine bottle from the top of the counter. "Take this and celebrate."

"Celebrate what?"

Rachel winked. "Whatever pops up."

"It's not even lunchtime."

"Live a little."

Nodding, Fleur left the shop and walked up the narrow street. Rachel's words lingered on her mind. *Live a little.*

Had she stopped living?

She frowned, cradling the wine bottle in the crook of her arm. She had promised her parents that she'd settle down on her return to Australia. But had she already begun? It came as a small shock that she didn't covet the nightlife she used to enjoy. Since starting the business, she found it fulfilled a part of her she didn't know existed. The shop satisfied her in ways that surprised her. Customers liked the atmosphere of the shop that she had created. They bought *her* cakes and pastries. All this was new to her. She was giving, she was appreciated.

The nights of partying until the sun came up and the days of traveling different countries, living out of a suitcase, waiting in airports, riding in squashed hot buses through towns that had no running water, going days without a shower all seemed like a distant memory.

And what amazed her even more was that she didn't miss it. She no longer wanted to meet guys at bars in out-of-the-way island resorts. She didn't want to pretend to enjoy their jokes or listen with interest to their crazy stories.

Why?

When had it all stopped being fun?

When had she become responsible?

How had she become a grownup without realizing it?

"Hey there, gorgeous."

Fleur blinked.

"Fleur?"

She turned, scowling, not focusing on the sleek car beside her. Dimly, she became aware of Patrick climbing out of his car and running around to her.

"Sweetheart? What's the matter?" His concerned blue eyes added to the tenderness of his voice.

She looked up at him. He was so lovely, so much Mr. Right that it frightened her.

I've fallen in love with Patrick.

Suddenly, she burst into tears.

Chapter Six

She cried harder as Patrick gathered her into his arms. The hardness of his body against hers and the smell of his wood-scented cologne filtered through her misery. She wanted to curl into him and have him hold her forever.

"I'll take you back to my flat, baby." He took the bottle of wine from her and guided her into the front passenger seat as gently as if she were made of porcelain.

They didn't talk on the short drive to his home and Fleur did her best to stem the tears and wipe her nose without drawing more attention.

Inside his flat she stood in the middle of the lounge room hugging herself while he shut the door and threw his keys onto the table by the door. Within seconds she was in his arms.

"What is it? Why are you crying?"

She shook her head against his chest, trying to think of anything else than that she loved this man who held her. Why did this have to happen now? When she was back home, that was the time for love, for finding a lifetime partner. Not here. Not now.

"Fleur. Speak to me." He walked her to the sofa and sat her on his lap. "Has something bad happened?"

"No, not really." She sniffed and looked away, gathering her scattered wits and thinking of what to tell him.

"Are you ill again?"

"No!" Horrified that she had panicked him so much, she kissed his cheek. "No, nothing like that."

"You gave me such a fright."

"I'm sorry." She smiled, a wan, teary smile. "Actually, I'm just being over emotional, ignore me. I'm sorry I gave you a scare like that."

"Is it something I've done or said?"

She stroked his cheek, mentally kicking herself for being so weak. "No, you have been wonderful. Please forget it. I have."

"Are you sure?"

She nodded and kissed him, snuggling in closer to his chest. At last she felt him relax and breathe easier.

"I was on my way to see you."

Remembering the flowers, she sat up. "The flowers you sent. Oh, Patrick, they are so beautiful. I can't thank you enough. You shouldn't have."

"They weren't the reason you were crying, were they?" He looked pale. "I didn't mean to upset you with the Australian flowers."

"You didn't, honestly. They are lovely."

He placed both hands on either side of her face and kissed her lips softly. "Were they too much?"

Fleur traced the outline of his mouth with her fingertip. "Yes, a little." She chuckled as he looked surprised. "But I love them. Thank you."

"I wanted to spoil you."

"You certainly did that. How did you find Australian natives?"

"Lord, it was a nightmare." He laughed. "It took a lot of planning, bribing and begging. The Internet is a wonderful invention."

"You shouldn't have gone to so much trouble."

"I wanted it to be individual and unique. Just as you are." He ran his hand up her arm and brought her closer to kiss her tenderly at first, then with rising zeal.

Many minutes later, Fleur leaned back to regain her breath and sighed happily. "Well, all I can say is thank you for making me feel special. I was overwhelmed. Rachel and a customer were quite speechless."

"The tongues will wag now, I guess."

She frowned a little. "Does that worry you?"

His hand slid up and down her thigh, sending quivers of pleasure to the very core of her body. He grinned. "Not at all. What about you?"

"No, I don't care. I'm not even known around here to any great extent so it doesn't bother me. Besides, I'm not going to be here forever." The moment she spoke those words her gaze flew to his and she died a little inside at his expression. What possessed her to say such an insensitive thing?

He tried to fob it off, but his smile didn't quite reach his eyes.

I've hurt him.

Guilt filled her, but the realization that he might feel something for her shocked her into stunned silence. Did his feelings go beyond the physical? They hadn't even slept together yet, but that was only a matter of time. And although sex was an important part of a relationship, it wasn't the whole thing and she wanted the complete package. Did he, too? If he did then their lives had just become a lot more complicated.

The thought formed and grew as she sat there nestled on his lap. A sense of belonging and closeness cloaked her like a warm blanket. This was exactly where she wanted to be—in his arms. Only, they lived on opposite sides of the world.

"Patrick, I'm sorry. I didn't mean to sound—"

"It's okay. I know what you meant." He pecked her nose and winked.

He caressed the back of her neck with his hand. "Can you stay a while? We can have something to eat."

She hesitated in further explaining what she'd said and meant. She didn't want to make a big issue out of nothing, but then she didn't want him to think she thought nothing of their relationship either. "I can stay an hour. Rachel is looking after the shop but I don't want to ruin our friendship by taking advantage of her good nature."

"She was a lucky find."

Fleur nodded. "Yes, very much."

Patrick bent and nibbled her earlobe. "There's plenty we can do in an hour."

Smiling, she wound her fingers through his dark hair and kissed him. "Show me then, my good man."

She laughed as he ravaged her neck and then pulled away to look into her eyes, his expression serious.

"Do you want the same thing I do?" His voice had deepened with need.

"Yes," she whispered against his mouth. Tingles of excitement and anticipation ran through her. Crazily, she wondered if she'd put on her good knickers or whether she wore her old ratty ones. The thought swiftly became redundant as he lurched to his feet with her in his arms. His strength stirred a primeval pride within her. Her man—the strong warrior claiming her as his mate. She giggled.

"Something amusing?" His lips quirked into a wry smile and his eyes darkened with unmasked lust.

"Not at all," she murmured. All laughter died in her throat and she was consumed with an ache of wanting that begged to be fulfilled. For a fleeting second a kind of nervousness blocked out her enthusiasm, but she quickly pushed it away and concentrated on Patrick.

He carried her across the room to an open doorway. She peeked in and saw his giant bed covered with a brown and gold duvet. The room was very masculine with mahogany furniture, but tasteful, if a little sparse in decoration.

Patrick paused and hugged her to him. "Are you sure, Fleur? I can stop now, if you want. There's no pressure."

Her heart melted at his gentleness and concern. She tightened her arms around his neck and softly kissed his lips. "I really want this, Patrick. I want us to make love and for a short time to pretend that nothing else exists outside your bedroom. Can we do that?"

His lips lingered on hers and she felt him smile. "For an hour, my gorgeous one, you'll not be able to think at all, but only feel."

"Sounds like heaven." She shivered with delight and eagerness and didn't give a fig for what type of knickers she wore.

He laid her on the bed, then stood back to take off his shirt and unbutton his jeans. She reached out for him and he quickly stretched his length alongside of her, taking her into his arms.

Fleur marveled in his hard body—a body worked into perfection by rigorous sessions at the gym. She ran her hands over the flat planes of his strong back and shoulders, enjoying the feel of him beneath her fingertips.

Patrick kissed her neck, nibbled her earlobes before moving to her mouth. His tongue flicked out and, as soft as a butterfly's touch, he tasted her lips. Heat grew like a gathering summer storm within her body. She squirmed as need, an intense ache, spiraled from the depth of her.

"Can I undress you, Fleur?"

She nodded, helping him to free her from the clothes that restricted them both. Growing more and more encouraged and bold, Fleur ran her hands over his penis that jutted out of his opened jeans. She ran her fingernails lightly along his length and Patrick gasped into her mouth. His hand slipped down between her legs and gently, with prolonged slowness, dipped inside her moistness. Sensations built as he caressed her, and not wanting him to experience any less pleasure than he was giving her, she hooked her thumbs under his jeans and underpants and wriggled them down. In the blink of an eye, Patrick kicked them off and rejoined her, crushing her against him so he could devour her in hot demanding kisses that sent her mind spinning and her body arching into him.

"I want to go slow, sweetheart, but it's hard. I want you so much..." he paused and grinned, "and it's been a while."

Fleur pulled his head down and kissed him. "We can go slower another time."

With this signal Patrick groaned and pressed her flat onto the bed. His knee nudged her legs apart and she became wet with anticipation of him entering her. She gripped his bottom and guided him into her, sighing as he filled and stretched her. It was the best feeling in the world. "You okay, darling?" Patrick asked, his face showing the strain of keeping rein on his actions.

"Yes," she whispered, nibbling on his lower lip.

He gathered her up hard against him and his thrusts became deeper and rhythmic. Fleur opened her legs wider, lifting her pelvis up to accept him fully as the magic began. He kissed her with each plunge, driving her up, higher and higher. She gripped him as waves of sensation built to fever pitch and then broke like starbursts to tumble over her. Her climax lingered as Patrick plunged to his own orgasm. She felt his body tense, the muscles of his bottom and back contracting before he momentarily suspended any movement and shuddered.

Slowly relaxing, it took him a second to focus on her and she smiled up at him cheekily. "Was that okay?"

He took his weight onto one elbow and gave her a long, sweet kiss. "It was bloody marvelous. What about you?"

A bubble of laughter rose in her chest. "Oh, I think I could suffer it again."

They shifted a little bit to fit more comfortably and when Patrick went to pull out of her, she stopped him. "No, stay inside me for a little while. It's nice."

"You sure?"

"Yes, absolutely."

The breeze, much stronger up on top of the cliff, lifted wisps of Fleur's hair as she stared out over the tranquil North Sea. To the left, Whitby township hugged each side of the River Esk, the numerous red-tiled roofs striking a sharp contrast to the surrounding green fields. The tide was in and many boats rode at anchor, bobbing gracefully.

Behind her the impressive ruins of the famous Whitby Abbey, silhouetted against the sky, held court to a flock of tourists. On this sunny day its medieval buildings didn't look too scary, despite all the Dracula stories connected to it.

Fleur sighed, admitting to her tiredness. She was burning the candle at both ends. Late nights with Patrick and long days at the shop. So far it was working out okay. They both had fun, enjoyed each other's company and mutually shied away from the subject of the future. Sometimes, in quiet moments like this, she felt as if she were riding on the crest of a large wave. The whole time she was on this happiness high she was wondering when the crash into the sand would happen. And happen it would. Each day brought her closer to her departure, edged her closer to an uncertain future with Patrick.

Did they have a future? Her heart said yes, her head said no, you're dreaming.

Patrick came from behind, wrapped his arms around her and kissed her temple. "I took some good photos. I've been living here for years and have never taken any local photos."

"That's a common occurrence."

"I suppose it is. Want to walk on to Robin Hood Bay?" He pointed to the right and the rocky cliff edges.

"How far is it?" She leaned back into his chest, so easy in his presence that it was like they'd known each other forever. "I'm only wearing sandals."

"About five miles." He squeezed her tighter, his voice dropping to a whisper. "Or we could go back to my flat."

She grinned, hearing the mischievousness in his tone without having to turn and look at the devilish expression she knew he wore. "You said we'd have an afternoon of sightseeing.

I imagined that meant shopping and walking along the beach or driving to the next town to visit some historical castle. Not hiking around cliffs in sandals."

He laughed. "And here I was thinking you were the adventurous kind."

She spun in his arms and reached up to wind her arms around his neck. "I've been on my feet every day all week—"

"And on your back every night—"

Fleur clamped her hand over his mouth and blushed as a tourist walked behind them. "Patrick."

He wiggled his eyebrows at her.

Ignoring his references to their nighttime activities, she continued, "As I was saying, after being on my feet all week the last thing I want to do is go hiking on my afternoon off. Besides, I've already climbed all those steps to get up here, which you insisted would be fun." She rolled her eyes at him. "As if."

He hitched her hips hard against his own. "Okay. No hiking." He kissed her lips and then looked all innocent. "We could go and explore The Dracula Experience shop."

Slapping his arm playfully, she dismissed his ridiculous idea. "No souvenir shops, thank you."

Patrick groaned, but took her hand and led her back to the path.

"You're a hard woman to please."

She leaned in closer. "Oh, I think you've worked out how to please me rather well."

Something flared in his eyes, something wild and passionate. Within a blink of an eye he'd grabbed her and ducked in behind a ruin. Backing her up against a stone wall, he held her face in his large hands and sweetly punished her with his mouth. Fleur arched into him as he used his tongue to build within her body an acute ache of wanting. Grinding his hips against hers, she felt his hardness, glorified in it, knowing that she had the power to make him hunger for her beyond all thought.

"Oh God, Fleur," he breathed hot against her mouth. His tongue flicked along hers and then he nibbled on her bottom lip as his fingers threaded through her hair. "You make me lose my mind."

She wiggled against him. Gripping his jean-clad bum, she pulled him in closer. The fire he stoked within her very center was near to boiling. In spite of them having made love each night for the last week, she couldn't get enough of him. He set her ablaze from a mere look of those gorgeous eyes.

A child's shriek shattered their cloud of lust and reminded them of where they were. Gradually the noise of tourists and a seagull's cry filtered through their absorption of each other.

Patrick smiled and carefully straightened her white blouse. "Shall we go get some ice cream?"

"I'd prefer to buy some Jet jewellery." At his scared expression, she grinned and rose on her toes to kiss him. "Don't look like that. It's my credit card not yours I'm using."

Fleur raced up the steps to the flat to the shrilling noise of the phone ringing. Throwing her bag on the sofa, she snatched up the receiver. "Hello?"

"Hello, darling."

"Mum." Fleur collapsed onto the sofa, smiling. "How are you?"

"Good, honey. You were a long time getting to the phone. Is everything all right?"

Fleur glanced at the clock on the wall. Five minutes to ten. She'd spent the whole afternoon and evening with Patrick, ending up in his bed. "Yes, sorry. I have only just got home. I could hear the phone from downstairs as I came in."

"You've been out?" Her mother's voice rose a tiny bit. "With Rachel who works for you?"

"No." She quickly changed the subject. "How come you're phoning again? We talked two days ago."

"Well I've some news."

"Good or bad?" Fleur frowned. She waited for her mother to continue and felt a sense of unease in her tone.

"Both."

"What's the bad news?"

Her mother's sigh reached across the miles. "Well, darling, your Uncle Harry had a stroke yesterday, but he's okay."

"Oh no." Fleur felt her heart somersault. She loved her Uncle Harry like a second father. It was he who showed her how bread was made in his shop. It was Harry who encouraged her to take a baking course after finishing school. "Mum, that's terrible. Is he all right?"

"He's doing good considering. You know he's never taken care of himself. The doctors say his body must have been giving him some warning signals, but knowing Harry he would have ignored them all."

"Will he recover though?"

"Yes, to some extent. He's lost some use of his left side."

"What about the shop?"

"He has assistants and a new trainee, who will have to learn even faster now. That shop is Harry's life and he'll be worried sick the entire time he's away from it."

"Shall I come home? I can work in the shop, that would ease his mind."

"No. Goodness, he'd be horrified to think he was the cause of you coming home early. Anyway, he's out of danger as far as I know. So don't panic."

"You sure?" Suddenly Fleur felt the sting of tears. She missed her family. She missed her way of life, of having barbeques on Sunday afternoons, watching the one-day cricket at the SCG, having big family dinners, which always included friends and neighbors. Despite all the times she had traveled, the little bits of home life were what always made her want to come home again.

"Yes, I'm sure. I'm going to the hospital shortly to see him."

"Give him my love, won't you?"

"Of course, darling."

"Okay." Fleur whipped a Kleenex out of its box and stuck it to her dripping nose. She didn't want to blow it and let her mother hear that she was crying. She tried to be cheerful. "You said there was good news, too?"

"Oh yes."

This time Fleur heard the happiness in her mother's voice and sagged against the cushions in relief.

"Your brother has announced his engagement to Susannah."

"No." Fleur shrieked like a school girl. "Oh my God, that is wonderful."

"I know. Your dad and I are so happy. Oh, Fleur, you should see the pair of them, they've got permanent smiles on their faces. Charlie even asked Susannah's father for permission before he popped the question. Can you imagine that?"

"He didn't." Fleur laughed, trying to imagine her crazy, good-hearted baby brother acting all courteous and romantic. "Did he go down on bended knee?"

"Yes. He took Susannah up to the top of the Sydney Point Tower and proposed there. The ring is beautiful. It's so exciting."

"He never mentioned a word of this to me." Uncharacteristically, Fleur felt for the first time the awful emotion of being left outside of the family. She had missed all these events—hadn't been there to share the devastating news of her Uncle Harry or the joyous excitement of her only sibling getting engaged. It hurt more than she thought possible.

"And guess what else?"

"Lord, hate to imagine." Fleur chuckled, kicking off her shoes and stretching her legs out along the sofa.

"They're getting married on Christmas Day!"

"No!" She stared at the phone as though her mother had spoken Hindu.

"Are you sure? How could they possibly arrange that?"

"Oh yes, I'm sure. Susannah has an aunt who's a celebrant and she said she'd marry them on Christmas Day in Susannah's parents' garden. You know how magnificent their garden is. It's always featured in the local open garden scheme, it's that beautiful."

"I can't believe it."

"I know. We're going to be so busy organizing everything. We're even tossing up the idea of having the reception here at our place because it will be difficult to get a venue for Christmas."

"Oh, Mum, that's a huge undertaking." Fleur thought of their rambling ranch-style home with wide verandahs and set on two acres. Two large fig trees dominated the backyard and beneath them swept dark green lawns that her father cared for as though they were centuries old Persian carpets.

"Well, true, but a marquee will fit in the backyard rather well and everyone can park their cars on the spare block of ground next door. Anyway, it's still being discussed."

"Right."

"So how have you been, darling?" Her mother's voice became concerned again. "Your health is okay? You're not doing too much I hope. You mustn't get run-down, my love. Are you eating properly?"

"I'm doing really excellently, Mum. Please don't worry."

"Of course I worry." Her mother sounded offended. "I've told you before, it's my job to worry."

"Well, I'm fine."

"You aren't short of money, are you? You must tell me or your dad if you are."

"I'm okay for money. The shop brings in enough to pay my bills and everything. The weather has been brilliant, really hot and so the tourists and day-trippers have been flocking here."

"So, you'll be staying for a few months more?"

Fleur smiled sadly at the touch of sorrow in her mother's voice. "Yes, Mum. It's only July. I've barely been here three months and I've got the shop lease until the end of September as you know. I can't break it."

"No, I guess not." Her mother sighed. "We all miss you a lot. It's like you've been gone for six months instead of three. This will be the longest you've been away at one stretch. Your dad said yesterday that he wanted you home. He misses his golf partner."

"He misses beating me, you mean." She laughed, but her laughter was edged with tears. She and her father had a special closeness and his tearful goodbye at the airport still made her throat tight with tears three months later. "I'll be home in October, Mum, not too long to wait."

"You promise?"

"I promise."

"I don't mean to be demanding, Fleur, really I don't."

"I know, Mum."

"It's just that we could easily have lost you with everything that happened, and well..."

"It's okay. I understand." She bit her lip, for her joy at going home and seeing her family was tempered with the sadness of leaving Patrick.

She had a life in Australia and deep inside her she knew she could never live in England permanently, even for Patrick. She'd be miserable if she did and it would crush her parents. Seeing them only once a year would sap her happiness, and besides, Australia was home. Its brightness, its way of life and spirit had made her what she was. She wanted her children to experience what she had in childhood. Safety, summer at the beach, hiking in the bush, playing netball on Saturday mornings, pool parties, the relaxed lifestyle that great weather gives you.

What about Patrick? that little voice of reason whispered.

Pain squeezed her heart. How was she to bear it?

Chapter Seven

Fleur pushed her hair back from her hot face and slid the two cups of coffee across the counter to the Japanese tourist. After taking the money and giving change, she turned to the next customer and took their order. The constant hum of voices, the coffee machine whirl, the opening and closing of the drink fridge all combined to fill the shop with noise, and Fleur had to lean forward to hear.

"We've run out of apple pies, Fleur." Rachel rushed by, balancing the last try of iced cupcakes, which she slid into the display counter. "There's nothing left in the kitchen and we're running low on soft drink cans."

"I know, and those tables need clearing." Fleur finished her customer's order and paused before taking the next one. "I can't believe how busy we are today. Is there something special happening in town?"

Rachel served a small boy who wanted to buy four cans of drink and ice creams. "We don't sell ice cream here, sorry. Do you still want the cans?" She collected his money and turned to Fleur. "I think there's some boating thing on down in the harbor."

A dark shadow passed by the shop's windows. They looked up to see an enormous bus coach crawl by. Fleur's eyes widened. "How on earth did that manage to drive along this narrow street?"

"He's obviously lost or new to the area." Rachel smiled as she served her next customer. "Let us hope he doesn't stop near here or this shop will become standing-room only."

The warmth left Fleur's face. "I don't have enough stock," she whispered out the side of her mouth as she bent, selected a jam tart from the display counter and placed it on the plate. She squeezed a dollop of fresh cream beside it, added a chocolate-dipped strawberry to the top and passed it to her customer.

"Do you know of any suppliers who will deliver on a Sunday?"

"No. None."

In a pause between serving, Rachel slipped out behind the counter to tidy the tables and carry the dirty crockery into the kitchenette, while Fleur made a quick list of the supplies they needed. They were short on many things. She bit her lip. Could she or Rachel be spared to run to the local supermarket? She cursed herself for not baking enough this morning.

"Ring Patrick," Rachel said, returning behind the counter. "He might have spare stock at the restaurant. Anything will do."

Fleur nodded and pulled her mobile out of her pocket. "He's doing paperwork today in his office."

She dialed the restaurant's number and Angela answered the phone. Frowning in surprise, Fleur stumbled a little over her words. "Oh. Angela? What are you doing there?"

"I work here."

Fleur bristled at her sharp tone. “The restaurant isn’t open.”

“Who *is* this?”

“It’s Fleur. Is Patrick there, please?”

“Of course he is, but he told me he didn’t want to be disturbed.”

“That doesn’t include me.” Seething, she had the urge to march up the hill to Donnelly’s and slap that woman’s smart mouth. “Can you transfer me to his office please?”

“Well…”

“Oh, forget it.” Fleur ended the call and dialed Patrick’s mobile. She should have done that in the first place.

“What’s going on?” Rachel gave her a quizzical look as she made fresh coffee.

“That bloody Angela trying to act superior.”

“I think she believed Patrick was her personal property until you came along.”

“Patrick told me he hasn’t dated anyone since coming to Whitby.”

“Doesn’t stop Miss Ice Queen Angela dreaming though, does it? I told you she had the hots for him.”

Fleur turned away as Patrick’s voice sounded. “Hi, babe, it’s me. I need your help.”

Within half an hour, Patrick was emptying the last box of soft drink cans into the shop’s fridge. His supplies had saved them somewhat, but the fresh cakes and pastries were all gone and Fleur was left serving packet biscuits with her tea and coffee. She’d have been embarrassed if she’d the time to think about it.

Afternoon heat kept the tourists and day-trippers in town, where they swarmed the ice-cream shops and tearooms looking for ways to keep cool. Despite the frantic pace of serving the hordes of people, Fleur couldn't help but smile every time she looked in the cash register and saw the money piling up.

"There, that's the last of it." Patrick collapsed the cardboard box and strolled around behind the counter.

"Thanks." Fleur flashed him a smile as she gave change to an exhausted young mother whose baby cried in its pram. The line of people wanting drinks and cups of tea stretched out between the tables.

Patrick placed his hand on her waist. "I can stay and help, if you want?"

For a moment she wanted nothing more than to sag into his arms, but a shop full of thirsty people were watching her every move. "I'd love it if you could stay for awhile."

He winked and then gave his attention to the elderly woman next in line. "It looks like I arrived at the right time. I get to serve this beautiful woman." The older woman blushed as Patrick turned on the charm.

Rachel groaned dramatically and Fleur laughed.

Much later, as the sun finally descended and dusk coated the town in gold and pink, Fleur locked the shop's door and leant her back against it. Her feet throbbed and her stomach growled with hunger.

"What a day." Rachel slouched across a table she'd just cleaned. "I'm so tired."

"I can't believe the amount of people we had in here today." Fleur pushed away from the door and helped her friend to her feet. "Go home and soak in a hot bath."

Smothering a yawn, Rachel flexed her shoulders. "I'm so glad Mum has Courtney tonight."

"Do you want me to order you some take-away?"

"No, thanks. Some toast and a cup of tea, bath and then bed. That's my plan."

From the counter where Fleur had stacked the profits, she picked up some pound notes and gave them to Rachel. "Here's a gift for all your help today."

Rachel looked at the money. "A hundred pounds? That's too much!"

"No it isn't and you deserved it."

"Are you sure?"

"I did well today, but without you I'd have been lost. I want you to have it and you can't refuse it." She smiled.

They walked into the kitchenette, where Patrick stood washing cups and plates.

"Thanks." Rachel hugged Fleur and then Patrick before heading to the back door. "Good night you two."

Left alone, Fleur stepped up behind Patrick, wrapped her arms around his waist and laid her cheek on his back. "Thank you for today. You were my knight in shining armor."

He swiveled around, and with wet soapy hands drew her close. "Have you the energy for me to be your knight in no armor?"

A warm sensuous heat filtered through her body, diminishing the tiredness. "I guess I could accommodate you."

He dabbed a blob of bubbles on her nose. "Why don't you go up and run a bath for us."

"I doubt we'll fit in it."

His blue eyes darkened and he bent to touch the tip of his tongue to her bottom lip. "It'll be fun trying though."

"Likely we'd end up in some weird position and have to be rescued by the fire brigade."

Patrick laughed. "And here I was thinking you were game for anything."

"I do have my limits and making the local newspaper's front page in some naked suggestive pose just isn't my style." As she went to kiss him, her stomach growled again. "Shall we order something to eat first? I'm starving."

"I'm starving too, sweetheart, but not for food, not yet."

Through his jeans, she felt his need pressing into her stomach. She reached up to bring his head down for a hot, urgent kiss.

Patrick groaned. "Fleur, if we don't stop now, I'll have you on this floor."

She laughed and tore herself away. On a wave of hot lust she floated upstairs and into the bathroom. She ran both taps and added lavender-scented bubble bath liquid and a few drops of scented oil. The aroma wafted on the steam and filled her nose.

She turned as Patrick stepped through the doorway.

"The washing up can wait." He grinned, pulling her to him and kissing her lightly.

"Shirking your duties?"

"I have other, more important duties to perform."

Fleur ran her fingers up his arms. "I like a man of many talents."

"I've yet to show you them all," he whispered.

Very slowly he hitched her shirt up over her head and threw the garment on the floor. His hands cupped her breasts, clad in a lacy white bra, and at the same time he nibbled her earlobe. His thumbs rubbed her nipples and she wondered hazily how she could have ever frozen from his exciting touch. Under his fingers, her skin sprang to life.

"I have to turn the water off..." Her limbs felt too heavy to move. She burned with wanting him, ached to have him fill her.

Patrick reached over, turned off the taps and then stripped off his clothes. As Fleur stroked his erection, he undressed her and kissed her with persistent need. Naked, they stepped into the bath, touching, caressing each other, using all their senses to reaffirm the link between them.

Patrick reclined against the tub and, with a mischievous glint in his eyes, grabbed her by the hips and guided her onto him. The fragrant steam encircled them, the hot water coating them with slick perspiration.

"Oh God, Patrick." She sighed, taking him into her core. A different hunger gripped her now.

In the muted soft lighting of Donnelly's restaurant, Fleur sat on a barstool and stifled a yawn.

"What can I get you to drink, Fleur?" Karl, the head bartender skillfully dashed a scoopful of ice into a tall glass and quirked his eyebrow at her. "Ask for something exotic, something lethal."

Fleur laughed. He was good-looking enough, and normally, in her other life, she would have enjoyed flirting with him, but since meeting Patrick she had no desire to play the game anymore. The knowledge both amazed and frightened her. "How about you surprise me?"

"That's the spirit!" He grinned, as he tossed a colorful concoction together. "Pun intended."

"That was bad." She shook her head, watching his skill. "A barman is supposed to know all the best jokes and one-liners."

He held up his hands. “I’m working on it, honest.”

“Perhaps you should buy a joke book?”

“Are you kidding?” Karl’s dark eyes widened. “That would be the kiss of death to a great barman such as myself.”

“You aren’t chatting up my girl, are you, Karl?” Patrick suddenly appeared at Fleur’s side, and as always her stomach flipped at his nearness. He gave her a quick kiss hello, and she inhaled his cologne and let her gaze absorb him. This evening he wore a navy suit with a white shirt and tie. In his hand he held his gold-rimmed glasses. He was sex on legs.

Karl flashed white teeth in a deeply suntanned face, placed a piece of pineapple on the edge of the tall glass, stuck a short straw in it and passed it to Fleur. “No, I decided not to hit her with the full force of my charms, which are irresistible to women of all ages.” He leaned in close to Fleur and wiggled his head with an exaggerated flourish like some hot Latino lover.

She waved him away playfully. “Oh, be still my beating heart.”

“Ahh…no woman can resist me.” Karl spoke with a false Spanish accent, took her hand and kissed it. “And because of this, I will withdraw my offer of a night of passion!” He winked suggestively. “I withdraw it also because if you threw over my boss for me, I’d lose my job.”

“Indeed you would.” Patrick pinned him with a predatory male glare that was only half teasing. “And then how would you pay for those weeks in Ibiza to top-up your tan?”

Karl’s smile faded and he was saved by the telephone ringing, which he promptly answered.

Fleur glanced at Patrick, frowning as she sipped her cocktail. “That was a bit rude.”

Rubbing a hand over his face, Patrick looked regretful. "Yes, it was. Sorry."

"I'm not the one to apologize to. What brought that on?"

"I've no idea."

"He was simply playing about, having a joke." Fleur shook her head at the foolishness of males.

Patrick gave her a wry grin. "I've not been jealous over a girl since high school, but seeing you and him laughing just hit me in the gut." His expression changed to one of puzzlement. "I made an arse out of myself, didn't I?"

"Yes, you did. So, it's a good job that I'm attracted to arses." She laughed up him.

He kissed her twice. "I'll go finish a few things and be right back."

"Speak to Karl first. He's a nice guy."

"Yes, he is and a good barman too. I'll tell him I was being a—"

"An arse?" she said, straight-faced.

"I was going to say a loser."

"That too."

Patrick leaned closer, his face inches from hers, his kissable lips within licking distance. "Don't forget, Miss Smart-mouth, you are sleeping with this particular loser."

She burst out laughing, earning a disapproving glare from Angela at the end of the bar. Fleur ran her fingers down Patrick's cheek in a loving caress, mischief running through her veins. "Even losers need to get laid once in a while, Mr. Donnelly."

Desire flared in his eyes. He grabbed her hand and opened his mouth to say something, but the door opened and an older couple entered the restaurant. Showing restraint, he smiled at her before squaring his shoulders and adjusting his tie. "I'll speak to you shortly."

"I hope you'll do more than just speak." She slipped her hand into Patrick's, delaying him. "Shall I wait here or at a table?"

"Here. I've just got to make a phone call and shut down my computer. Can you wait another five minutes and then we can have a drink together."

"That's if Karl isn't too scared to serve you."

"Oh, very funny." He grabbed a menu book from the stack further along the bar and gave it to her. "Look over the menu and decide what you want."

She laid the menu on the bar. "It doesn't matter if we run late and miss the movie. I can drool over George Clooney another time."

"We'll make it. I wouldn't want to be responsible for you not getting your weekly dose of drool."

She pinched his bottom. "I'm sure I can find other things to entertain me."

His eyes narrowed and darkened with heat. "Keep that thought," he whispered.

Once he'd gone back to his office, Fleur gazed around at the scattered diners. It was early, not yet six-thirty, but there were a few couples in and a small family group. The phone never stopped ringing and she heard Karl and Angela taking reservations.

She and Patrick were supposed to be having a quick dinner and then going to the movies, but she'd had such a busy day again that she doubted she could stay awake until the end of the movie—even for George Clooney.

She yawned again, hiding it behind her hand as Angela walked through the bar carrying a tray of glasses that she placed underneath the counter. Her thin smile seemed pasted to her face.

Fleur yawned once more, a huge yawn that made her eyes water. Lord, she'd fall asleep in her dinner if she wasn't careful.

"Are you bored with us here at Donnelly's?" Angela asked, wiping down the bar top.

"Not at all." Fleur straightened on the stool and gave her a cool look. "It's just that I've been up since four this morning baking for the shop and then serving all day."

"Oh yes, your little shop." Angela's tone was dismissive, as though Fleur's business meant nothing or was something beneath her notice.

Seething, Fleur tilted her head to study the other woman, wondering if she'd been a bitch since school or was it a later development. Some women turned into complete witches as a result of bad relationships or rejection. Some girls were born catty, and others started puberty as sweet girls and came out the other end as bitches with attitude.

Fleur had escaped that particular trait but had been on the receiving end of it a few times in her life. She'd never been the one who had to have the right makeup or the most expensive brand of clothes. Thankfully, she'd been popular at school with both the girls and boys and her closest friends were a bit tomboyish like her too, which helped when Fleur preferred playing football than giggling over teen magazines.

"You must be missing home?" Angela's assessing eyes glinted like ice. "I mean, you have no one here that's family and all that. So, you must get lonely."

"I have Patrick, how could I possibly be lonely?"

"Of course, but then that's not a proper relationship, is it?"

Confused at the statement, Fleur swirled the straw around in her glass. She was trying very hard to not take offense with this woman, but it was damn hard. "Why isn't it?"

Loftily, as though she held all the answers, Angela twitched one shoulder, her manner superior. "Well, it's a passing fancy, isn't it? A holiday fling. We all have them and forget about them as soon as we arrive home."

Fleur forced herself to smile, to act uncaring as the hideous words pierced the defensive barriers around her heart. "I can't predict the future, but a holiday fling this is not."

"You think that now..."

"I know it."

"Time will tell, I guess. After all, long-distance relationships never work, do they? That is why couples end holiday flings on the last day, with no promises, leaving them free again."

"I'll not be leaving Patrick free." Fleur swore silently in her head at this woman's needling darts of poison.

"You're not?" Angela pouted. "That's a bit selfish, isn't it? I mean, Patrick should be allowed to be happy once you've gone."

Oh yes, and you think you're the one to make him so.

Fleur gripped her glass, stifling the urge to throw it at Angela's self-righteous expression. "Perhaps you should ask Patrick what he wants. His answer might surprise you."

"And it could surprise *you* too."

"I doubt it."

"You know, I really like Patrick and, to tell you the truth, if he asked me I would sleep with him." Angela's lips thinned into a semblance of a smile as she sauntered away to answer the phone that rang at the other end of the bar.

There. Now the truth was out. Fleur nodded, even managed a chuckle. The poor woman was in denial about Patrick and her. She thought she still had a chance with him.

A fleeting thought of "what happens when I do go home?" crossed her mind, but she ignored it. She was too tired to think of the future tonight. Besides, if Patrick had wanted to sleep with Angela, he could've done it by now.

Out the corner of her eye, Fleur saw Patrick leave the service area and head towards her. At the same time a group of people entered the restaurant and Angela guided them to a nearby table.

"I spoke with Karl. It's unanimous; I'm a pathetic arse doubling as a sad loser." Patrick sniffed with mock disappointment and sat on the barstool beside her.

"You have a rare talent, Mr. Donnelly."

"Thank you." He kissed her and leant back. "What did you choose for dinner?"

"I didn't," she murmured, watching Angela hand out menus to the new arrivals. She actually felt a little sorry for her. It would be hell to be in lust with someone who didn't feel the same way. The waitress was pretty and could be more attractive if she lost the sour expression she always wore.

"What's the matter?"

Fleur glanced at Patrick. "Are you aware that Angela is in love with you?"

He frowned. "I don't think she is. Why do you say that?"

"Women's intuition and some heavy hints on her part."

He shook his head. "I'm not interested in her, never have been."

Fleur blinked and chose her words carefully. "But you knew she was interested in you?"

"I had an idea she was." He shrugged. "She isn't important to me."

"She doesn't have to be important to you for you to have a one-night stand."

"That's not my style. I've never encouraged her in any way. She works for me and is good at her job, as far as I'm concerned that's all there is to it." Patrick scanned the filling restaurant, nodded hello to a few guests and checked his watch. "You aren't concerned about Angela, are you?"

"No." Fleur looked at him. "I have no need to be, do I?"

"Absolutely not."

An elderly man came to the bar to order some drinks and Patrick smiled and welcomed him to Donnelly's. Karl was serving another couple and Angela was waiting the tables. Patrick glanced at his watch. "The rest of the staff should be arriving in the next ten minutes. It's busy tonight. Karl said they've taken eight bookings so far."

She couldn't give a rat's backside about the staff. She wanted to dig a little deeper about Angela and one-night stands. "So, the fact that Angela told me she would sleep with you if you asked her doesn't bother you in the slightest?"

Patrick had just waved to a friend arriving with his family yet, at Fleur's words, he slowly turned to stare at her. "What did you say?"

"Nothing." She hopped off the barstool and grabbed her bag. "Shall we find a table?"

"Listen to me. Angela, or any other woman for that matter, doesn't interest me in the slightest"—his voice dropped to a whisper—"even if they offered themselves to me lying naked, smothered in honey on top of a red Ferrari, I'd turn them down."

Fleur nibbled her bottom lip, and despite the passing restaurant patrons she couldn't resist teasing. "So, that's your fantasy, is it? A naked woman smothered in honey lying on a red Ferrari."

Patrick tilted his head in thought. "Nah, on second thoughts scrap the honey. It'd only ruin the paintwork."

In full view of everyone, she kissed him.

Chapter Eight

Fleur swished the mop under the tables without much enthusiasm. Tiredness pulled at her bones, making closing-up time a lengthy procedure. Weeks of late nights in Patrick's arms and early mornings getting up to bake were catching up on her. Plus it was that time of the month. Usually her periods were three-day affairs that didn't cause her too much bother but this month her stomach was bloated and she just felt like crap.

Outside, evening was drawing in, the crowds going home after another eventful day of sightseeing. The day's trade had been a good one. The weather hadn't been brilliant with low clouds and scattered rain showers, which had sent customers into the shop for a cuppa and cake. Both she and Rachel worked nonstop until about three o'clock when finally there was a lull in trade and they could sit down and rest.

Dunking the mop in the bucket of soapy water, she absentmindedly gazed out of the window, her thoughts miles away from the boring chore at hand. Patrick had called at lunchtime to say he was on his way home from Manchester where he'd been for the last two days supervising the work at the new restaurant. She'd missed him, but the time apart had let her catch up on paperwork and the large amount of ironing that irritated her every time she walked into the bedroom. The problem with wanting to look her best for Patrick and working in the shop meant all the clothes she wore were "good" clothes that needed ironing. Ironing was the devil's own revenge.

A sharp knocking on the door snapped her out of daydreaming about Patrick. Fleur propped the mop against the wall and unlocked the shop door.

On the footpath stood an elderly woman dressed in a blue summer's dress and black cardigan with a small green trolley beside her. "Hello there, dearie."

"Hello." Fleur smiled. "The shop's closed, I'm afraid."

"Oh that's all right, I'm not here for anything. In fact I've brought some books for you. I'm Dawn, and live a few streets back." The older woman bent to lift back the flap of the trolley, revealing a stack of musty-smelling books. "I don't want them anymore as I'm moving into a retirement home and there isn't room to swing a cat in the room I'm having there."

"Oh, I see." Fleur stepped closer for a better view.

"Barbara Cartland most of them." Dawn nodded. Then, peering around the street as if searching for spies, she beckoned for Fleur to lean in nearer and whispered, "Underneath there's a few modern romances. You know the sort." She gave a big wink. "I had to clear them out before my daughter saw them. She'd have a heart attack if she knew I read the *steamier* sort."

Fleur grinned. "I bet she would."

The elderly woman straightened and laughed. "Give me a man who knows what's he's doing and I'm happy." She sighed and stared down at the books. "It's been a while since I sampled a good man, so my books are all I have to keep me young."

Biting her lip to stop from laughing, Fleur winked. "I'm partial to a good man myself."

"Well, there's plenty in there, my pet." Dawn pointed an arthritic finger at the trolley.

Fleur looked up from the books to a familiar hottie walking towards them.

Patrick.

She touched the other woman's arm. "See that gorgeous guy?"

"Oh, my, yes indeed." Dawn adjusted her glasses and gave him the once-over. "Rather a fine specimen."

"Absolutely." Fleur took a deep breath, drinking in the sight of him. He walked with an easy stride, head up, shoulders back. Confident. Powerful. Today he wore a dark grey suit and a light blue shirt, the tie gone. After him being away for two days, her body suddenly forgot it was tired and her blood thumped along her veins with renewed vigor. She had missed him like hell.

"I certainly wouldn't kick him out of bed on a cold night," Dawn spoke seriously.

Spluttering with laughter, Fleur covered her mouth with her hand. Dawn must be eighty if a day.

Patrick, smiling, walked straight up to Fleur, hugged her to his side and planted a kiss on her temple. "Hello, beautiful."

"Nay, you never said he was actually yours." Dawn's eyes widened. "I thought we were window-shopping."

Chuckling, and lightheaded on love, Fleur shook her head. "Sorry, I've already purchased."

Patrick frowned in puzzlement.

Dawn sniffed and gave him another once-over. "Aye well, I think you've spent your money wisely."

Fleur's cheeks ached from holding in her grin. The older woman was a character, the type of Englishwoman she admired. Forcing herself to be serious, she indicated to the trolley. "How much do you want for them?"

"Nay, I don't want your brass, lass." Dawn dismissed with a wave of her hand. "They're that old most of them that you'll have to give them away, too."

Unhappy at getting something for nothing from such a delightful old lady, Fleur made a compromise. "Okay, how about I give you a free coffee or tea with a piece of cake when you next drop by?"

"Deal." Dawn smiled. "Here, take me trolley too and that'll save you unpacking them now. I'll pick it up in the morning before I start me shopping. All right?"

"Sure." Fleur smiled, took the trolley handle and pulled it up the step. "See you tomorrow then."

"Aye." Satisfied, Dawn traipsed away back up the street.

Inside the shop, Fleur placed the trolley in the kitchenette and returned to Patrick, who quickly gathered her into his arms.

"Hello you."

"Hello yourself." She ran her hands over his shoulders. He felt so good. Solid. Warm. Hers.

"I missed you." He kissed her soundly, holding her so tight she couldn't breathe and she loved it.

"And I missed you." She threaded her fingers through his hair that was in need of a cut. "How was it in Manchester?"

"Good. Everything is going to plan. I'd like you to see the new restaurant. It's looking good."

"Me too, but I can't get away from here for a whole day." She stifled a yawn behind her hand.

His expression became sad. "You work too much."

Fleur rested her head against his shoulder and closed her eyes. “I don’t see it as work. I’m enjoying it, and meeting characters like Dawn makes it that much more special. This was what I came here to experience. To get the feel of how my ancestors lived.”

“I know, but you must get enough rest, too.”

“Yes, sir.”

He nibbled the end of her nose and then planted a light kiss on it.

“Want to go upstairs?”

She slapped his arm playfully. “Is that all you think about?”

He tilted his head and frowned as if in deep thought. “I think it might be.”

“Oh you.” She sprang out of his arms, laughing. “I’ve got to finish mopping. Not all of us have minions to do the dirty work for us.”

“My minions happen to adore me,” he said in an exaggerated upper-crust accent, then winking, he slouched back against the counter. “Actually, I haven’t been to the restaurant yet. I should do that now so then we’ve got all night together.”

Fleur paused, and a warmth crept into her cheeks. “Um, Patrick... There’s a slight hiccup about tonight.”

“Oh?”

“We can’t make love.”

He pushed himself away from the counter and came to her. “Why?”

Embarrassment filled her. “Because I have my period.”

His eyes softened, he reached for her waist and brought her to him. "That's a pain. I've been away for two days and I'm rather hot for you, sweetheart."

"Sorry."

Patrick grinned. "As you Aussies say, 'no worries'."

"It doesn't mean we can't still be together though."

"My thoughts exactly," he whispered, descending for another sweet kiss. His tongue traced the shape of her lips as his hand moved down over her breast to tease the nipple, which instantly hardened under his caress. He left a fiery trail of kisses down her throat, and shifting her shirt away, he nipped and sucked at the tender flesh along her collarbone before returning to kiss her with a deep hunger.

After he let her up for air, she smiled and moved back to the mop.

"We can get take-away and a movie if you want."

"Sounds good to me. I'll bring it back with me. Chinese will do?"

"Yep. Excellent. I've got some egg custard tarts left over, too, for dessert."

Patrick walked towards the door. "I'll be back at seven o'clock."

With a final kiss, he left her to her cleaning. Fleur sighed in contentment. The more she saw of Patrick, the deeper in love she fell. How was she going to leave him—actually get on a plane and fly away from his arms? Her heart fluttered in protest at the mere thought. Perhaps there was some drug she could get from a doctor to help her through it? Heartbreak pills. Was there such a thing? Pills for leaving-the-man-you-love syndrome.

The mopping finished, she tipped the dirty water out of the back door and left the mop to dry. In the corner of the kitchenette, Dawn's green trolley waited for her attention, but the thought of soaking in a nice hot bath won the battle over dusty old Barbara Cartland books.

Sighing, she wiped a weary hand over her eyes. She had an hour before Patrick returned and, as much as she loved him and had missed him in the last two days he'd been away, she longed for an early night.

Flexing the exhaustion from her neck, she climbed the stairs and summoned the energy to make herself look nice for him. An hour to wash her hair, scent her skin and find her comfiest tracksuit. She giggled. The way she was feeling, a soft tracksuit, chocolate and a bottle of wine would be heavenly right now. Patrick had seen her mopping the floor, wearing no makeup, and knew of her current intimate bodily functions—he could cope with her wearing a tracksuit.

The noise of the pub blasted Fleur as she walked into the smoky main bar area. A jukebox in the corner playing a Tom Jones song competed with the talking, laughing and yelling of the people enjoying a night out in one of England's busiest cities, Manchester.

Fleur held Patrick's hand as he weaved them through the throng edging the bar. Behind her Phillip and Jane Donnelly followed. Jane was talking nonstop to Fleur, but the crush of the crowd made it difficult for conversation.

Finally, Patrick squeezed his body between two beefy, hard-looking men and found a vacant table near the gent's toilets. He hustled Fleur and his mother in behind the table. "Not the best part of the pub, sorry." He grimaced at the men filing in and out of the toilet door.

"Beggars can't be choosers, love." Jane smiled. "Here is fine. In fact anywhere we are is marvelous when we're together."

"Where's Dad?"

Jane adjusted her blue skirt and tucked her bag down by her feet. "He stopped at the bar to get the drinks. You know what he's like. Go help him or we'll die of thirst waiting while he talks to everyone."

"He never changes." With a sigh of the condemned, Patrick turned and threaded his way back through the crush. Fleur grinned, watching him go.

"I say, this is my kind of pub, old and homely," Jane said, raising her voice to be heard. "I care nothing for those modern places with their bright lights and blaring rock music. The ones that are all steel and glass seem so cold and sterile. Who could have fun in such a place?"

Agreeing, Fleur looked around at the aged décor. It was a small pub, situated in a back street that Patrick knew, and not far from his new restaurant. The interior did need a makeover, however, the old world charm of the place made you feel at home, comfortable.

"Wasn't dinner lovely? A nice place to eat, too. I don't usually eat Italian food. It's a shame Patrick's restaurant wasn't ready for us to eat there."

"Perhaps we can do this again, when the restaurant is open."

"That would be fantastic. I've had a grand day today." Jane sighed happily. "Meeting you was wonderful and seeing Patrick full of enthusiasm once again."

"Yes, it has been a great day." Fleur paused as a drunken man swayed towards them, obviously heading for the toilets. He was singing at the top of his voice, and only the door closing behind him muffled the racket he made. She turned back to Jane. "I really wanted to visit the site of Patrick's Manchester restaurant and being introduced to you and Phillip was a bonus."

"We are so proud of Patrick. He has the talent and business sense to be successful. Did he tell you of his dream to own a chain of restaurants?"

"Yes, he did."

"Well, he would have done it too, if it wasn't for the trash he married. Good riddance to her, that's all I can say." Her bright blue eyes sparkled as she grinned at Fleur and squeezed her hand. "You're just the kind of woman I wanted Patrick to meet. I'm very happy he finally has."

Fleur smiled, grateful that Patrick's parents were lovely wholesome people. She'd been nervous at first, meeting them this morning, but their friendliness soon put her at ease. Jane and Phillip had taken her to heart. Their friendliness had blown away any unease and before long she had felt like she'd known them for years. "Thank you."

"His first wife, Julie, never liked us you see. She thought herself a cut above us and didn't visit often." Jane shrugged, her small frame stiff with disapproval. "Not that I minded, like. My ex-daughter-in-law was a rather large pain in the butt to have as a guest. She hated my house, which is nothing grand, simply a semi-detached in a normal neighborhood street. I think she was very disappointed when she first saw it."

Fleur remained quiet, not knowing what to say. Julie wasn't a topic of conversation she often had with Patrick, not because either of them was uncomfortable to broach it, but because she simply didn't feature in their day-to-day lives. She knew that Patrick no longer harbored any love for his former wife and he had moved on from that relationship.

"Oh I know I can speak plainly with you. I know you're not one of those yuppie people as she was. You're normal."

Totally relaxed with Jane, Fleur chuckled. Yuppie she was not. Yet, she liked being called normal after spending her life being different. Her wandering ways now seemed another lifetime.

"All I ever wanted for Patrick was a nice normal girl to love. I can't tell how worried I've been over him."

"Oh? Why?"

Jane tucked a strand of dark hair behind her ear and sighed. "I thought that Julie had ruined him, had turned him into a bitter man whose heart had shriveled up and died."

"I think he was a little bitter..." Fleur searched the crowd for sign of the one they talked about, but Jane patted her hand, getting her attention again.

"Even if you and he don't last more than this summer, I'll still hold you dear to my heart because you showed him how unsuitable Julie was and you've also shown him he deserved more. He's a good man and deserves to be happy. It's been years since he's shown an interest in anyone and I didn't want him to spend his life alone."

"Your son is very special to me. I'd like to think we'd last longer than this summer, but everything is so uncertain..."

Jane smiled a sad smile that gave a glimpse of her younger, wistful beauty. "Life is uncertain, Fleur, that's why you have to grab at it with both hands."

Fleur nodded. "I mean to. I've been given a second chance and I don't intend to waste it."

"Patrick needs you in his life."

"And I need him."

"Then you're halfway there." She glanced up, saw husband and son returning and immediately sparkled with life again. "Where have you been, making the stuff?"

Phillip, barrel-chested and full of fun, plonked two drinks down on the table. "Nay, my love, I was chatting up the barmaid." He fished a scrap of paper out of his shirt pocket. "Got her phone number too!"

Jane, as quick as lightning, grabbed the piece of paper and read it. "Oh aye, Phil Donnelly, sure you have, my love. The lady has indeed written something for you." Jane laughed, nudging Fleur. "It says 'You're a dirty old man, go home to your wife and beg for her forgiveness!"

Phil's ruddy face paled and he sat on a short stool with a plop. "She never wrote that."

Fleur looked at Patrick, who shook his head in despair and passed the drinks around. "Dad's been chatting up barmaids for as long as I can remember."

Phil puffed himself up importantly and smoothed down his silver hair. "I had to show the lad how to do it proper like, don't I?"

Patrick, sipping his beer, nearly choked. "Yes, Dad, you've shown me all right. You showed me how *not* to pick up a woman."

"Get away with yourself, man. You've learnt from the master." Phil winked at Fleur. "How else would you know how to grab a cracker like Fleur here?"

"Sure I did, Dad." Patrick rolled his eyes. "Actually, I think if a barmaid ever took up his offer, he'd have a heart attack on the spot."

Jane rocked with suppressed giggles. "Aye, and so would the girl if she ever saw him undressed."

Phil roared with laughter, leant over and planted a smacking kiss on his wife's lips. "Ahh, my Jane, you'll do for me, girl."

Patrick took Fleur's hand and gave her a wry smile. "Welcome to my crazy family."

The shrill sound of the phone ringing gradually brought Fleur out of a deep sleep. Her limbs felt as heavy as lead. Frowning, she realized that Patrick had slipped out of bed and padded into the other room to answer it.

The slight headache made her scowl as she staggered up and found her satin dressing gown. She picked up her watch from the bedside table and, waiting for her eyes to focus, she finally made out the time. Five a.m.

Five a.m?

Who rang at this time, for God's sake?

"Fleur it's for you," Patrick said, all sleep tousled and sexy in navy boxers. "It's your mother, and she doesn't sound happy that I answered the phone. Sorry." He crawled back into bed and threw his arm over his eyes.

"Yes, darling, you look very sorry." Sarcasm was an easy asset when you'd been sleeping on less hours than a baby with colic for the last two days.

She plodded over to the phone and licked some life back into her dry lips. Her mouth felt like someone had used it as a bar's slop tray. She was out of practice for partying late. "Mum?"

"*Who* was that?" Her mother's outraged voice shocked Fleur into wakefulness.

"Patrick."

"Patrick who? Are you sleeping with him? How long has this been going on?"

"Mum, calm down. I'm nearly thirty years old, for heaven's sake. Not some teenager."

"Where have you been? I've been ringing for twenty-four hours. I was just about to ring the police or Australia House or someone."

Fleur held the phone away from her ear to reduce the damage her mother's shouting would do to her hearing. This kind of behavior totally surprised her. Never had her mother acted this way. She was Valerie Stanthorpe—high-school teacher, dependable in a crisis and could cook a mean roast lamb dinner—not this raving loony on the other end of the phone.

"Mum, everything is fine. I spent the day with Patrick. His parents came for a quick visit to England and we went and saw them in Manchester and then went out for dinner and drinks afterwards." *A very late dinner and drinks.* Phillip and Jane Donnelly knew how to have a good time and insisted on buying drinks for her until throwing-out time.

"And you didn't think to let us know in case we tried to call. You've been telling us you're never away from the shop and so what were we to expect?"

"Mum—"

"Anything could have happened to you and how would we know? We're on the other side of the world."

"Rachel opened the shop for me. What's going on, Mum? You're never like this."

"I've never been as frightened as this. I didn't know what had happened to you. Why didn't you take your mobile?"

"I accidentally forgot it." Reaching over to the kitchen bench, she grabbed her old bag and pulled out her mobile.

Twenty-four missed calls.

Guilt clawed at Fleur's insides like a wild animal. "I was rushing around before we left to make sure Rachel had everything she needed and then I swapped bags and just forgot all about it."

"Well, that's not smart, Fleur."

Fleur's stomach clenched at hearing the tears in her mother's voice.

"I know. Sorry. Why were you calling me? Is everything all right?"

"Harry."

Fleur closed her eyes and gripped the phone tighter, instantly knowing the truth. "He died."

"Yes, darling. I'm so sorry to have to tell you over the phone."

"When?"

"Two nights ago. August third. On his birthday."

"When is the funeral?"

"Next Monday."

Fleur nodded and swallowed back tears. She'd be crying soon enough without starting now and it'd be more than just Harry she'd be crying for because she'd have to go home, leave Patrick. This tragedy would have shaken the family. Harry was very much loved.

Her mother, calmer now, talked quietly. "There's no pressure to come home."

"You know I adored Uncle Harry."

"Yes, of course, but he'd know how hard it would be for you to leave now with the shop and everything."

"I cannot miss saying goodbye to him, Mum." Fleur felt herself weaken on the tear front and quickly drew in a shuddering breath. Patrick, concern written on his face, came to her and wrapped his arms around her waist. She gave him a small smile and leaned on him as her mother spoke.

"Your dad and I will pay for you to come over and then fly back again. Could you manage that? Close the shop or something?"

"Yes, I'll work something out."

"Okay then, love. Ring me when you've planned what you need to do."

"I will. Bye, Mum. Love you." Fleur replaced the receiver back on its cradle and sighed.

"What's going on?" Patrick's low tone was full of concern.

"My Uncle Harry died." Fleur rubbed her forehead, dazed. The words didn't make it seem real. She couldn't really absorb the reality of her much-loved uncle being dead. She pictured Harry's happy face and booming laughter. Her family was so close it would be impossible to have a function and not include Harry. He had witnessed so many events of her life. Learning to swim, winning the netball grand-final in year six, high-school graduation, learning to drive, buying her first car, meeting her first boyfriend. The list was endless.

Patrick had become very still. "Are you going home?"

Fleur looked up at him, loving his strong jawline, the softness of his blue eyes and his sensual lips. Her heart sank to her toes as she nodded. "I have to. I must say goodbye to him."

"Of course." His smile was restrained and he moved away towards the kitchen. "Want a cup of tea or some breakfast?"

"Actually, no, I won't, thanks." Fleur headed for the bedroom. "I need to wash and dress. I've got so much to do."

"Will you close the shop?" Patrick leaned against the doorjamb.

In the bedroom, she opened drawers, looking for something to wear, but what would she need? Would she get a flight today? She trod on her slinky black dress lying on the floor that only hours before Patrick had stripped from her in the frenzied heat of passion.

"I'll have to talk to Rachel. But I can't expect her to do more than she has. She looked after the shop all day yesterday. I haven't spoken to her to see how that went yet. I'm neglecting her and the shop. I can't be rude and ask for more of her time. Besides there'll be no cakes or anything to sell with coffees. That doesn't look good."

Fleur groaned, trying to think what to do first.

Clean underwear.

At this moment she would offer big money for a proper shower. It was another thing she missed about home. Having baths were slow and tedious when in a hurry. There was nothing like a hot shower to quickly wash your hair in the morning. But the flat was outdated and a small narrow bath was the best she could do right now. Back in May, when she first arrived, it had been a novelty to have a bath all the time, now it was a hindrance.

Patrick collected his clothes. He shrugged on his shirt and then his trousers. One of his shoes was by the door, the other under the bed. "I'll head home and shower, but I'll call you later. Okay?"

Shower. Patrick had a modern bathroom, but the time it would take to go to his place and back she could have a bath.

Her gaze lingered on his flexing muscles. Muscles that she had kissed and licked last night in a mind-blowing night of love. Only last night his body had been soft, relaxed. Now tension radiated from him, his expression preoccupied, worried.

What was he thinking? Was he seeing a glimpse of how their future could be with one of them always on a plane? Her stomach twisted. This would be their first goodbye. No doubt the first of many and she hated the thought.

For a fleeting second she panicked. She couldn't do it. She couldn't leave him. Then she remembered to breathe and common sense prevailed once more. It would be fine. They'd been apart for a few days already when Patrick went to Manchester. Now it was her turn to go away for a few days, but she'd be back and they could spend some more months together and then, later, much later, they'd decide what to do for the best.

Patrick found his phone and keys and placed them in his pocket before pulling her into his arms and kissing her tenderly. "Let me know what plans you make. I can take you to the airport."

"I'll let you know once I've booked my flight." Fleur smiled and held him tight for a moment longer. She had the scary feeling that everything was slowly disintegrating before her eyes and she didn't know how to stop it. "I'll only be gone a few days."

Rubbing his nose against hers, he sighed. "I hope so."

Chapter Nine

Fleur clicked on the seat belt and looked out the window. Below, Sydney Harbour dazzled in all its magnificent splendor. The plane banked, dipping the wing on Fleur's side as if to give her a better view. She smiled to herself. Home.

No matter how many times she had flown into Sydney it always gave her a thrill to see the Harbour Bridge and Opera House. Ferries crossed the harbour and cars buzzed along the streets. Everything in miniature. Even the August weather—winter—was wonderful and welcoming, the sky an intense blue and clear of clouds.

As they descended a little more, she glanced at her traveling neighbor. Finn the hippy. A man whom, despite his grungy appearance, was rather pleasant to talk to. He wore no shoes, said he didn't even own a pair, and Fleur wondered when he'd last washed his dreadlocks, but delving into his personal hygiene was something that her mind repelled from. At least his long white shirt and torn jeans were clean or cleaner than his revolting feet anyways.

Finn flashed her a grin, his eyes wide and bright. "Nearly there."

She smiled in reply. An hour before he'd been a little edgy, quiet, and at their last meal she noticed his hands shook. However, after a trip to the toilet—and he was gone a dreadful long time—he seemed better, happier, cheerful. An awful thought entered her head. *Dope.* Fleur blinked and out the corner of her eye tried to look for traces of some sort of drug. It was always her luck to get the weirdos next to her. One time, on the way to Bali, she was seated next to a fat guy who talked and mumbled to himself for the entire flight. And then there was the time, on a flight to South America, she got a young woman who decided to tell Fleur her life story complete with tears and foul language. She once had a guy next to her who totally ignored her and elbowed her each time he moved and didn't apologize.

"Have you got someone meeting you?" Finn asked, beaming like a ray of sunshine.

"Yes. My parents." Fleur inched away from him, hoping to God that no trace of Finn's drug had drifted onto her. Minuscule powder grains would be impossible to see to the naked eye. Those cute sniffer dogs suddenly became a serious issue. She dusted off her khaki three-quarter pants and swore under her breath. The urge to jump up and run to the toilet was strong, but she could hardly walk off the plane stripped down to her underwear.

With a bump they touched down on the runway and sped past the airport buildings. Fleur sighed in relief. She was safely home.

An hour later, after making sure she stood as far away from Finn as possible when he went through customs, she exited the arrivals gate and looked frantically for her parents. Tears filled her eyes despite the rush of excitement at seeing them again.

"Fleur."

She twirled, her heart bursting, to see her father, John, dodging through the crowd to her. "Dad."

"Hello, love." He swooped her into a hug. "How are you?"

"Good. You okay?" She sniffed, feeling silly at crying like a baby at her age. "Where's Mum?"

"Oh, she went to get a bottle of water and no sooner had she left I saw you come out." He took the luggage from her and she stared at the extra grey in his hair and close-clipped beard. She'd only been away for three and a half months but they suddenly seemed like years. It was as though a large gap had opened up, splitting her from the hub of the family life. The feeling wasn't good. In fact, she hated it.

"Val," her dad called, having spotted her mum near the exit door.

Her mother saw them and rushed over. "Fleur."

Fleur was hugged tightly once more and again tears spilled over her lashes. "How are you, Mum?"

"I'm a thousand times better now you're home." Valerie Stanthorpe wasn't very tall, but she made up for it in energy and efficiency. Today she looked smart in a beige pantsuit with her light brown hair neatly trimmed in a shoulder-length bob.

Fleur smiled and kissed her cheek. "You've lost weight."

Her dad snorted. "Yes, well, she's done nothing but worry over you and then Harry. She's not sleeping properly either."

Fleur raised her eyebrows at her mum in query. "You don't want to make yourself sick."

"It's nothing. Your dad exaggerates. Silly man." Linking her arm through Fleur's, her mum drew them out of the airport and towards the car park. "Did you have a good flight?"

"It was okay as they go. Too long as always." A blast of fresh air hit Fleur full on the moment they were out of the air-conditioned building. "How's Charlie?"

"He's good." Val smiled. "He should be home from work by the time we get there."

They crossed the road and John took the lead in finding the row their car was parked in.

"The funeral is tomorrow." Her mum sighed, the sorrow deep in her voice.

Fleur nodded. "I made it in time then. Good."

"There's something else, too," Val whispered and suddenly John stopped and turned.

"Val, we agreed not to mention anything until we were back home."

Puzzled, Fleur looked from one to the other. "What is it?"

Patrick slowed down the car as he passed Fleur's shop. Through rain lashing the car window he made out Rachel standing near a table, serving some customers. He toyed with the idea of stopping and going in. Would Rachel think he was checking up on her? He wasn't of course. He simply wanted to be surrounded by things linked with Fleur.

A car's horn tooted behind him and that decided it for him. He swerved over to the side and parked the car. The rain increased the moment he exited the car and he swore. He was sick to death of rain.

"Hello, Patrick." Rachel greeted him from behind the counter with a warm smile as he entered the shop.

"Hi, Rachel." He smiled at her and shook the rain from his hair. Suddenly, being in the shop hit him like a lightning bolt between the ribs.

Fleur. He missed her so much. What had possessed him to come in? Everywhere he looked there were touches of Fleur. The hundreds of books she lovingly stocked the shelves with, the slender vases of flowers on each table, the elegance of the country shabby chic furniture. It all made his ache for her deepen. Christ, he was a fool to expect this would make him feel better.

"You miss her too?" Rachel's expression looked like he felt.

"God yes." He sat on a stool by the counter. The shop wasn't busy, just an older couple by the window drinking tea, and he was glad of it.

"Want a cup of tea or coffee?"

"Coffee would be great." Patrick glanced at the bare display shelves beneath the counter; usually they were filled with Fleur's sugary delights.

"Have you been busy?"

"No." Rachel shook her head and set about making the coffee. "All this rain we've had this week has kept the numbers down. I'm worried about the profits. Without the extra people and not able to sell cakes and stuff the shop doesn't make much."

"Right." He could see she was worried and felt awful for her. "Fleur won't be that bothered I don't think. She's got other stuff on her plate to worry about at the moment. This place was only a hobby for her."

"Maybe so, but still, it looks bad." She passed the coffee to him.

"Yesterday I was asked whether we sell hot food because it was so cold. Bloody weather. It had to rain once she left, didn't it? It makes me look bad."

"Don't worry about it." He gave her a wry smile. "Hot food would be the answer for winter."

"Yes, but Fleur won't be here in the winter." Rachel's expression was downright miserable. "I hate her not being here.

It's like I've known her all my life. I don't know how I'll cope when she leaves for good."

"Me either."

Her gaze became quizzical. "Are you two serious then?" She placed her hand over her mouth. "Sorry. That's none of my business."

"I don't mind you asking. She's met my parents now so I'd like to think we are serious." He grinned, silently pleading with all the gods and fates to make it so. Being without her was just wrong. He couldn't describe it any other way. Fleur made him whole.

"Have you had any news from her?"

Patrick sighed and remembered their conversation last night. "I talked to her briefly last night, but they had company and she couldn't talk long."

Rachel nodded and absentmindedly wiped the counter with a blue cloth. "I haven't spoken to her since she rang me after the funeral, telling me her news."

"Being left Harry's bakery and the building it's housed in was a huge shock to her. Now she's got a heap of legal stuff to sort out. Who knows when she'll be back." His stomach clenched just thinking about it. Fleur had responsibilities now, a business, staff, property. What did she have to come back for?

Me.

But am I enough? He had the sinking feeling that he wasn't.

Fleur sat at the kitchen table, the cup of coffee going cold in her hand. With a fingernail she followed the tablecloth's pattern. Outside the magpies called out their morning greeting and the sun, slowly climbing, promised another fine day.

Silence pervaded the house. Her parents still slept. It was a good time to think.

She sighed. It seemed all she had done since arriving back home two weeks ago was think. In front of her sat a cream manila folder full of documents denoting her claim to her Uncle Harry's bakery, goods and stock, and the building it occupied including the apartment above it.

Yesterday she had gone there, to the bakery, which under the head baker was still open and trading for business. The staff, saddened by Harry's death and known to her, welcomed her with open arms. The gap Harry left was hard to fill. His presence was everywhere—his booming laughter floating on the air. She hardly remembered the conversations, because standing in the middle of the shop had brought it home to her. All of it was hers—a successful, long-standing business in the main street of Camden.

She was so frightened by the realization that at one point she couldn't breathe. How on earth could she live up to Harry's expectations? She had no idea he'd leave her such a gift. She felt honored, humbled and terribly scared. That he trusted his most prized possession into her hands floored her. He knew her history of never sticking to one thing for longer than five minutes. The whole family knew she only worked long enough to save the money for a ticket to travel to another country. She had never shown the urge for stability, never known or wanted it.

Until now.

Until Patrick.

Opening the shop in Whitby, enjoying the responsibility had awoken her to a whole new life. A life she liked. And being with Patrick had also uncovered a new need for a deeper kind of relationship.

"Good morning, love." Her dad walked into the kitchen, scratching his tousled hair, and going behind her, he switched on the kettle.

"Morning." She smiled as he patted her shoulder. "Sleep well?"

"Not too bad." He took a mug out of the cupboard. "You been up long?"

"No," she lied. Her parents worried enough about her without her sleeplessness adding to it.

"I'm making a pot of tea. Do you want some?"

"That would be lovely." Fleur turned and gave him her cold coffee to pour down the sink. "I'll put the toast on." She rose from the chair and went to the bench. After putting four slices of bread into the toaster, she collected the butter and blackberry jam from the fridge and the vegemite and peanut butter from the pantry.

Her dad placed the sugar bowl and milk on the table. "What are your plans for today?"

"Not sure."

"Are you going to the shop?" The kettle boiled and he switched it off and poured the water into the teapot.

"I don't think so. They don't need me."

"Nonsense." He frowned at her. "You're the boss now. You have to take over the running of it."

"I can't go in and start throwing my weight around five minutes after Harry's gone." The toast popped and she placed the slices on two plates and brought them to the table.

"I didn't say to do that."

Fleur sighed. A growing headache didn't make her feel any better either. She buttered the toast and passed two slices to her dad. "It's all so much to take in, Dad. It scares me."

"That's only natural, love." He spread vegemite onto his toast. A look of sympathy lit his hazel eyes. "Harry knew you could do this. He had faith in you. Leaving you the bakery meant giving you a financial future."

"I know, and I'm grateful, really I am. But I didn't expect this." Fleur tore the toast in half and bit on it without really tasting it. The bakery tied her to home and the weight of responsibility hung heavy around her neck.

"Whether you expected it or not is immaterial now. You have it. It's up to you what you do with it."

"I'm not a baker, Dad." She knew her tone was defensive, but couldn't help it. "I took a pastry course at college and worked part-time in Harry's shop. That doesn't qualify me as a baker."

"No, it doesn't. But you do have a qualified baker in Neil Price. Harry wouldn't have given him the job if he weren't good. Plus there are two apprentices. You won't need to actually bake yourself unless you want to."

She threw her toast down in frustration. "You don't understand. It's not just about me baking bread and cakes. It's the whole concept. It's a thriving business and what do I know about taking care of staff and wages and insurances?"

His expression became puzzled. "Aren't you doing that now in Whitby?"

"No. It's a tiny coffee shop in a small tourist town. It's something I just wanted to do for six months, and then I'd pack up and come home. I'd give the books to charity, send the equipment back to the dealers and hand the keys over to the landlord. Simple."

"But it's still given you the idea of what's required at the bakery. There's not much difference between the two except the size."

Fleur leaned back in the chair and played with her toast. "There's more difference than that, Dad, and you know it."

"What, you mean being tied down and held accountable?" He snorted and shook his head. "Are you telling me my daughter, the sassy, smart kid who's toured the world, who has helped build schools in third world countries and backpacked across places most people have never even heard of, can't settle down? Can't live up to the legacy of her uncle or his trust? Is that what you're telling me?"

The condemnation in his voice made her lift her chin in defiance. Her stomach clenched. She had let him down and to see that in his eyes hurt. Hurt bad.

Her dad gently put down his knife, which altered her to the way he was thinking and feeling. Her father never banged and slammed things in temper. Instead he did the opposite and kept his anger in check by concentrating on each movement he made. His quietness used to frighten Fleur and her brother much more than a raised voice ever did and they would know they were in serious trouble. Sometimes she wished she was a child again, when the most important decisions in life were going to the cinema with friends and choosing which movie to watch.

"Fleur."

She looked up into his eyes.

"You know your mother and I support you in your decisions, even when we don't agree with them."

She nodded, remembering the odd clashes they had over her choice of country to visit; countries that, although beautiful, weren't always safe. "I know."

"You told us that after spending the summer in England you would want to settle down." He reached across the table and patted her hand. "Have you changed you mind about that?"

She shook her head and tears clogged her throat. "No. I haven't changed my mind. I do want to settle down..."

"But?"

Fleur sighed, her headache pounded her skull and her heart somersaulted at the thought of Patrick.

Her dad stood and picked up his plate and cup. "I don't think you know what you want." His gaze softened. "You never did."

After he'd left the kitchen, Fleur let the tears silently fall. Did she disappoint her parents? Had they been waiting for her to grow up for nearly thirty years? They were wrong. She knew what she wanted. Patrick. Patrick, who lived on the other side of the world.

Rising, she went out the back sliding door and walked across the patio. She couldn't stem the tears and her vision of the backyard blurred.

"Fleur?" Her mother stood in the doorway tying the belt of her pink dressing gown. Her eyes widened in alarm. "What is it? Why are you crying?"

Wiping the moisture from her face, Fleur sniffed and blinked. The desire to laugh wildly hit her and she bit her lip to prevent such absurdity. "You'll never guess, Mum."

"What?" Her mother came to stand beside her and wrapped her arms around her waist.

"I have fallen in love." A shudder shook her and her head felt ready to burst. "Dad's just been going on at me for not wanting to settle down and face my responsibilities and yet that's all I want to do. But I can't."

"Why?"

"Because Patrick lives in England and my life is here."

"Are you sure you love him? A proper love, I mean. A deep love that will last through the bad times."

Fleur nodded. Just thinking about him made her stomach flip and her heart thump. "My feelings for him are that strong. I've never felt that way before about anyone."

"And his feelings?"

Shrugging, Fleur dropped her gaze. "I think they could be, but naturally he's holding back because he doesn't know if I'm staying around."

Her mother took a deep breath. "You could always sell the bakery and move to England for good."

"I suppose..." Fleur smiled lovingly. She knew how much that cost her mother to say. She wiped her face again. Damn tears! She hated crying. How wretched could falling in love and inheriting a business be, for crying out loud.

"You know what I think, darling?"

Fleur gazed at her, knowing that mother-knows-best tone. "I'm sure you'll tell me." She sniffed and desperately needed a handkerchief, which her mum promptly provided from the deep pockets of her dressing gown. Mothers.

"Well, I think you've finally realized you have to stop running away and being as free as a bird and it frightens you witless. You're spoilt, Fleur. Always have been. Everything's been too easy for you."

Horrified at her mother's words, Fleur stepped back out of her arms. "That's not true."

"Isn't it?" Val Stanthorpe tutted and folded her arms across her chest, ready for battle. "You've spent your whole life doing exactly what you pleased."

"You encouraged Charlie and me to do what makes us happy," Fleur accused, hating her mother's ability to always get to the heart of the matter instantly. Her father never did that. He tiptoed around anything painful or sensitive, slowly drawing the confession or secret out without you realizing it. Her mother had the subtleness of a sledgehammer.

"Your father and I always want your happiness, there's no question about it. That's not the point. The point is you have never needed to grow up."

"I don't believe this." Fleur twisted away. As if she didn't feel rotten enough. Now she was being chastised like a teenager.

"For the first time in your life you've been given an opportunity to be accountable for the decisions you make and you hate it. You hate having other people relying on you, depending on you. But you can't run away to the middle of Africa this time, Fleur, and pretend it isn't happening."

"You know nothing about me."

"Oh, darling." Val laughed. "I know you better than you know yourself."

"I don't run away!"

"Yes, you do. The minute you found out you had cancer, you were planning to leave here. You couldn't wait for the operation and chemotherapy to be finished with so you could pack your bags and disappear again."

Fleur glanced back over her shoulder to glare at her mother. "Planning the whole Whitby shop thing kept my spirits up and kept me from dwelling on the fact that cancer was in my body."

"It also kept you from facing it."

"That's a lie." Fleur spun to face her. Why was she bringing all this back up? She didn't need this now. "Why are you doing this, Mum? I don't want to think of that time."

"No, you never do. You hide it away, run from it. Just like you're running from the responsibilities Harry has given you. Did you ever think what it's been like for us, Fleur?"

"What do you mean?"

"The very day you got the all clear from the doctors, you left the country. For months beforehand you cared for nothing but your plans to leave, to follow your own purpose." Tears glistened in her mother's eyes. "Did you once think about your father and I? About how we felt? We didn't even have time to be thankful for the chance of having you healthy and safe again before you were gone. My mother died of breast cancer when I was only twenty, before she'd seen me marry. You knew that, yet you didn't stop and consider how I was feeling. How scared I was that I would lose you too."

Stunned, Fleur stared at her mother, whose grief was clearly visible. Had she done that? Left without a thought to her parents' concern? She couldn't believe it. Had she been that heartless?

Yes. Yes, because she had been so frightened about dying she couldn't deal with another's worries. She had survived because of her determination to blot out everything except getting better—getting better and leaving. In another country she could pretend that cancer and doctors and hospitals didn't exist. For a time she could be free and untroubled...

"Fleur, I'm sorry. I shouldn't have said all that." Her mother stepped forward hesitantly.

"No, Mum, it's me that's sorry." Fleur's voice broke on a sob and she ran into her mother's arms.

Chapter Ten

Fleur hitched her bag over her shoulder and tried to find the right key. The soft drizzle hadn't stopped falling since she landed at Manchester airport four hours ago. She shivered with cold. Why was it that international flights had to land at dawn, which then forced you to be tired all day and suddenly unable to sleep that night? Jet lag was Mother Nature's revenge for being up where you don't belong.

Driving into Whitby on a dull grey morning wasn't welcoming. She'd left warm sunshine for this. No, not for weather, obviously, for that would be stupid, but for Patrick. She hadn't even left home for the shop—it was no longer important. It had only been Patrick that brought her back. She'd come back to pack up the shop and to talk to Patrick about their future. To see if they had one or not.

Her constant phoning of Patrick's mobile only to get his voice mail deepened her bad mood. The last she heard from him was three days ago and she could tell from his tone that their separation hadn't been easy for him. He had been short with her, distracted. When she questioned him, he'd replied he had problems with the new restaurant in Manchester, then he asked when was she coming back and she couldn't give him a straight answer because at that time she didn't know. She had things to sort out, plans to make about the bakery and her taking over it. Then, shortly after their conversation finished, she told her parents that she was returning to England to close the shop. The next day she was on a plane.

Now she was here and desperate to see him, to reassure herself that they were good together.

Three weeks. She'd been out of his arms for three weeks. Insufferable.

Fleur finally opened the door and walked inside. She placed her bag on the kitchenette's bench and peered around the wall into the shop itself.

Nothing.

She frowned. Why wasn't the shop open? Where was Rachel?

Checking her watch again, she read five past ten. Business hours were nine to six. Fleur stepped behind the counter. Everything was clean and neat, but the air of abandonment irked her. Without the sunlight, the noise of the coffee machine and the chattering of the customers, the shop seemed dead. Uncared for.

Back in the kitchenette, Fleur grabbed her mobile and then went outside and up the stairs to Rachel's door. She knocked three times and waited. She couldn't hear any movement and knocked again. Nothing.

She rang Rachel's number and heard the phone ringing inside. She tried Rachel's mobile and it rang straight to her message bank.

First Patrick now Rachel. Where was everyone?

Plodding back down the stairs, she entered the kitchenette and went straight up to the flat. The living room smelt musty, damp. Had it been raining the whole time she was away? She turned on the hot water heater. A bath would be heavenly right now. The idea of soaking for an hour was delicious.

Just then she heard a car door slam. Running to the window, she looked down and saw Rachel and Courtney climb out of their car.

At last!

Swiftly, Fleur ran downstairs and out into the yard. "Rachel."

Surprised, Rachel spun around. "Fleur!"

They hugged each other in the rain and laughed.

"When did you get back?"

"Ten minutes ago." Fleur led them both back in the shop. "I've been trying to ring you."

Rachel held Courtney close and the little girl seemed a bit peaky. "I'm sorry, Fleur. My mobile was cut off. I was behind on paying it. It's been a bad week. I'm sorry I couldn't open the shop this week."

"Has something happened?"

Nodding, Rachel sighed and glanced down at Courtney. "This one's been in hospital all week with some virus. She couldn't keep anything down and in the end they had to put a drip in her so she wouldn't dehydrate."

"Oh, no." Fleur crouched down and caressed Courtney's cheek. "Are you better now, sweetheart?"

"Yes." Courtney nodded, but dark smudges under her eyes told another story.

"Poor pet." Fleur stood again and smiled in sympathy at Rachel.

"Must have been tough for you."

"It was. It all happened so fast. I didn't know what to do for her. It was scary. I never want to go through that again." She sighed deeply, the worried look still in her eyes. "And then I was worried about the shop, but I couldn't leave Courtney—"

"No, of course you couldn't. It didn't matter." Fleur touched Rachel's arm in understanding. "Courtney is far more important."

Rachel's chin quivered. "But you trusted me to keep it going."

Fleur hugged her friend, feeling guilty for leaving her to care for the shop when she had a young child. "I'm the one who's sorry. I shouldn't have given you the burden of running the shop. I was wrong. Stupid."

Rachel gave her a watery smile. "God, it's been awful here without you. It's done nothing but rain and the most dreadful gale force winds. The tourist numbers have dropped and some days it wasn't worth opening and then when Courtney started getting sick Mum came over to help out."

"I feel terrible about all this. Oh, Rachel, I'm so sorry." Fleur clasped her hands together, tormented by guilt. "I never expected to be away for so long. Three days I thought, not three weeks."

Stroking Courtney's head, Rachel tucked a strand of hair behind her ear. "I have to get this one up into bed. Want to come over and have a cup of tea?"

"Sounds good. Give me ten minutes. I want to have a wash and change my clothes. I was going to have a bath, but I can do that later. You wouldn't believe my luck. I was seated next to this woman who didn't believe in deodorant." Fleur shook her head at her bad fortune in the seating neighbors she had on planes. She was seriously considering booking two seats for herself from now on.

Twenty minutes later Fleur was sipping a relaxing cup of tea with Rachel. Courtney, still recovering from her illness, was tucked up in bed fast asleep.

For a while Rachel did all the talking, mostly about Courtney being in hospital and the fright it gave her. But by the time the packet of chocolate biscuits was half empty, the conversation turned to other things.

"So, how does it feel to be a property owner then?" Rachel grinned.

"Weird." Fleur studied the few drops of tea left in the bottom of her cup. "Confronting, actually. My whole trip home was confronting."

"Lord, that sounds deep." Rachel chuckled.

"It was." Fleur sighed, recalling the long chats in to the night she had with her mother. They'd been able to air their thoughts, worries and dreams, and at the end of it found a new closeness.

"Have you spoken to Patrick?" Rachel asked, reaching for another biscuit.

"I've been trying his mobile since I got off the plane, but no answer."

"He's in Manchester."

"Why?" Fleur's stomach clenched. He hadn't told her. It was more than just distance that separated them now. He was slowly withdrawing from her. Before she left to go home, he'd call her every day even if he was seeing her that night, but not any longer. The first week in Australia it had been once a day, the second week, every second day and the third week every third or fourth day. It hurt. Just like she knew it would.

Rachel shrugged. "A problem with the new restaurant. I think it's a major problem actually from what he told me.

Something to do with a crumbling inner wall and water pipes leaking in the ceiling or something like that."

A spark of the green-eyed monster appeared. Fleur's tone changed and she couldn't help it. "You saw him a lot while I was away?"

Rachel's eyes widened. "What do you mean?"

"Well, you seem to know—"

"Lord, Fleur, don't tell me you're jealous?" Rachel laughed.

Fleur stiffened, feeling stupid and irritated at the same time. "No..."

"You are." Rachel laughed louder and then remembering that Courtney slept, put her hand over her mouth. "You silly woman." She lightly punched Fleur on the upper arm. "You're mad, you know that?"

Fleur just looked at her, waiting for the resentment to die, which it would of course. Already common sense worked its way past the lump of ridiculous envy. None of this was Rachel's fault. She knew it, accepted it, but still her heart wouldn't listen.

"Patrick adores you. He missed you really badly. He'd come into the shop to moon around as if you were going to appear any minute." Rachel shook her head. "Did you not know how he felt about you?"

"Not really." Fleur rubbed her eyes, feeling foolish. That Patrick had feelings for her only made the situation worse. The thought of saying goodbye to him was like a stab to the heart. "This is all so hard, Rachel. It was insane to start this relationship. What the hell possessed me?"

"Patrick?" Rachel winked.

Yes, Patrick possessed her in every way and she loved it even if it did drive her crazy.

"I think you love him."

Fleur nodded. "Yes, I do."

"What are you going to do then?"

Fleur thought of her mum and dad, of Charlie's wedding, Harry's bakery, the staff, the apartment above the shop and the life waiting for her back home. "I'm closing the shop, breaking my lease and going back home."

Stunned, Rachel stared. "What about Patrick?"

"Well, that we still have to sort out." Fleur felt sick just thinking about it.

Rachel shook her head. "We need wine or something. Something to drown our sorrows with. I hate the thought of you going." Her eyes glittered with unshed tears. "I'll miss you."

"And I'll miss you, too." Fleur reached over and hugged her. "This whole experience wouldn't have been as great as it was without you. Thank you."

"Thank you for letting me be a part of it." Rachel wiped her nose and sniffed. "When do you leave?"

"In a few days." Fleur unfolded her legs and stood. Yawning, she rubbed her eyes. "I've got to speak with the landlord and tell him I'm breaking my lease and all the rest of it."

Rachel yawned as well. "Lord, I'm tired. You can never sleep in hospitals."

"Why don't you lie down for an hour while Courtney's asleep? You'll feel better."

"Yes, I might do that." Rachel walked with her to the door. "It'll be a shame to not have the shop open again."

"I know." Sadness descended on her like a heavy weight. This week would be a week of goodbyes and misery. "I'd best go and have a bath before I start organizing the shop's closure."

"I'll come over later and give you a hand if you want."

"Lovely." Nodding, Fleur kissed her cheek and left the flat.

Once inside her own flat again, she went into the bathroom and ran the bath, adding plenty of lavender-scented crystals. The last time she'd used these crystals was when Patrick lay on her bed dozing after a wonderful meal at the restaurant and an hour of sensual lovemaking. Slumped on the edge of the bath, Fleur let the tears fall. She'd never be able to smell the scent of lavender again without thinking of that night.

Patrick swore long and hard. With an angry glance at the speeding fine lying on the passenger seat beside him, he swore again. He'd not had a speeding fine since he was a teenager. Well, it served him right. There was no point screaming down the highway and getting himself killed, he'd not see Fleur any faster doing it *that* way.

He snapped off the radio. The blathering DJ irritated him. What a week. What a bloody god-awful week. Surely nothing more could go wrong. Problems, major problems at the new restaurant threatened his sanity, especially when he was trying so hard to keep it together, to stay cool.

And to top it all off, after a stressful meeting with a brain-dead builder, who he'd like to punch into next week, he had been about to read his messages when he dropped his mobile and it smashed to smithereens. Never in the history of mobiles had a mobile phone shattered into as many pieces as this one did. Even if he'd hit it with a hammer he couldn't have disintegrated it as well as what that small drop had done. Bizarre.

Hence his speeding to Whitby to see her. Hence his disgust at being pulled over by a policeman with an attitude. Of course he knew speeding was dangerous and of course he knew speeding in the rain was suicidal. But Fleur had left messages—messages he couldn't answer.

Fleur.

That she was back in the country had him as excited as a dog in a butcher's shop. She never left his mind. Always there waiting for him to weaken and think of her. He didn't want to think of her while she was gone. He'd been desperate not to because when he did his heart thudded like an old-fashioned threshing machine. Did all men feel like this or was he getting soft? This experience was new to him and one that he wasn't comfortable with. Julie had never made him feel like this.

Patrick frowned. Had he ever loved Julie? The answer evaded him. He cared for her at the beginning, and he didn't want anything bad to happen to her now, but his feelings for Fleur knocked him for six. He had a suspicion she was "the" one, but how did a man know, for Christ's sake? Did one go on gut feeling? Thinking back, he'd not gone on gut instinct with Julie. With her he had gone with the flow. It seemed easy, expected, uncomplicated, and in the end, boring.

But not this time. His relationship with Fleur was none of those things.

Scary.

He slowed down and turned off the A174 and onto the road leading into Whitby. After another right and then left, he was soon parking his car behind Fleur's shop. The sight of her small white car made him grin.

He'd missed her.

After locking the car, he went to the back door and pressed the buzzer. Minutes ticked by. He pressed it again. Above him Rachel stepped out onto the top of the stairs, smiling.

"Hi, Patrick. You know she's back?"

"Hi. Yes, got her messages. But she's not answering."

Rachel grinned and winked. "Likely in the bath. Is the door open?"

Patrick tried the handle and it turned easily. "Yes."

"She'd be expecting me, I said I'd pop over later, but since you're here I'll not bother." She winked. "See ya."

He raised his hand in acknowledgment and then ran up the stairs. The door to the flat was closed but not locked. Silly woman. Anyone could've just walked in.

He called out, not wanting to frighten her. "Fleur? It's Patrick."

"I'm in the bath, hang on." Her muffled voice came from behind the bathroom door.

For a moment he considered joining her, he ached to touch her, but he hesitated. Three weeks stood between them. Three weeks in which she could've changed her mind about him. Separations didn't always make the heart grow fonder. Sometimes it made the person wake up and want to run a mile in the other direction. Which had happened with Fleur? Damn.

Striding over to the kitchen, he tried not to be anxious. In a way it was like starting all over again. Would she want a kiss hello, a cuddle? What would she say? What would he say? *This is crap.* He didn't want to feel awkward.

Nervous energy had him switching on the kettle, setting the cups out on the kitchen bench. He should have brought her something. Flowers, chocolate, anything. Why didn't he bring her something? All he'd gotten was a speeding fine. Damn.

He couldn't stand this insecurity, this lack of self-confidence. How on earth had he changed from being confident and assured of his future? If this was how it would be after each time they were apart then he couldn't do it. No way. Not again. Not for him all this worry, he'd end up with an ulcer.

"Hello there."

He spun around and sucked in a breath. She stood by the wall wearing jeans and a pink long sleeve shirt that had the top three buttons undone, revealing a white flimsy lacy thing underneath. An ache spread through him. Damp strands of hair clung to her face. She wore no makeup and looked fresh and warm. Only her green eyes held him still for they showed her uncertainty. *So, she feels as insecure as I do.* That was some comfort.

"I've put the kettle on." He groaned. What the hell made him say that?

"That's good. I'd like a coffee." She tucked her hands behind her back and seemed set to cry.

Bloody hell.

"Did you have a good flight?"

She nodded and smiled. Pushing herself away from the wall, she went to sit at the kitchen bench. "How have you been?"

"Fine."

"Rachel told me there's been problems at the new restaurant?"

The kettle clicked off and he turned to pour out the water. "Yes. I can't believe it. We were one week from opening when the ceiling collapsed. Apparently there was a split pipe in the ceiling, it burst and the weight of the water brought the ceiling down. I'd told the builder to make sure everything was okay and if it wasn't to call in any tradesman needed to fix it. He assured me nothing was wrong. Idiot."

"Sounds like you've had a rough time of it lately."

You don't know the half of it.

Patrick passed her the coffee mug and the bowl of sugar. "I'm sure it'll be all sorted by the end of this week. The builder promised to work long hours to get it done, but we had to push back the opening day for a couple of weeks."

She glanced up from under her lashes at him and Patrick stopped breathing. *She is lovely.*

Fleur turned away. "Shall we sit down?"

"No."

She stopped and stared at him.

He sighed deeply. This wasn't fun. "Fleur, we're being awkward with each other and I hate it."

Her eyes reddened with tears. "I know, me too."

"We've always been honest with each other so talk to me. Tell me what you're feeling, thinking, because I can't cope not knowing."

She shrugged one shoulder and her chin wobbled. "I can't say the words."

His heart was smashing into pieces much better than his phone did. Excellent. Patrick straightened his shoulders, preparing for the hurt to come, and said the words for her. "You're leaving for good."

She nodded and a single tear ran down her cheek.

Nope, he wasn't doing this.

He wasn't having this pain.

"I'm sorry," she whispered.

"Well, we knew it would happen one day, didn't we? At the picnic we talked about it." He concentrated on being businesslike and in control.

"Doesn't make it any easier."

"No." He pushed his hands into his trouser pockets. "We should have stopped it that day, at the picnic. It was stupid to continue."

Her eyes widened and she thrust out her chin in defiance. "And missed all the days between then and now? No. I'm not sorry we didn't end it then. We've had a great few months. I'd rather that than nothing at all."

"Yes, but it would have been easier to walk away back then."

"Perhaps."

Patrick swallowed and took a deep breath. "Well, I'd better go."

"I was thinking though." She paused to wipe her tears and he died a little death at the action. "I was thinking that maybe we could stay in touch... Um... I'd like to..."

He shook his head, rejecting the idea immediately. "No."

Fleur's startled expression exposed her hurt but he couldn't weaken, couldn't subject himself to be a part-time lover. He wanted all or nothing. Simple as that. When he'd started to think that way he had no idea, but he just knew that one day he'd like kids, a house, maybe a dog. But that wasn't possible when your partner lived in another country.

"I'm sorry, Fleur, but I don't think that's a good idea." He walked into the sitting room heading towards the door. Escaping this was the only thing on his mind. If being in the land of the living meant experiencing pain of this magnitude then he'd rather be the dormant bachelor he was four months ago.

"Why?"

Patrick stopped and closed his eyes. "Because I can't."

"Can't what?" Her voice grew stronger, edged with anger. "There are no rules here, Patrick. No one says we have to stop knowing each other the minute I leave Whitby."

"I say it." He fed off her anger, preferring that emotion to the gut-wrenching ache that filled him. "I don't want to only see you once or twice a year."

"There are emails and phones. We can—"

"That's no relationship, Fleur." He snorted derisively. "I don't want that at all. You're killing me now, how long do you think I'd last doing this year after year? It's not normal, not right. Couples have to be together."

"I'm sorry. I was just—"

"Prolonging the agony?" He raised his eyebrows. Suddenly his anger grew into a tormented rage at her selfishness. How dare she do this to him? "You didn't want to say goodbye, did you? Maybe you preferred to do it in an email at a later date?"

"No!" Her eyes flew wide. "That's not it at all. I—"

"Isn't it? What about all your plans for marriage and children? Wouldn't that be a tad hard to do when you've got a boyfriend on the other side of the world?" He very badly wanted to destroy something. He had to get out of here. His chest felt fit to burst with all he wanted to say but couldn't. Stuff this for a joke.

"Patrick—"

"I have to go."

She stamped her foot. "Will you let me finish just one sentence?"

Annoyed, he folded his arms and waited.

For a long moment she glared at him and then slowly the stiffness left her body, and like a trodden-on flower, she crumpled to her knees before him.

In an instant he was kneeling on the floor beside her, crushing her to him, feeling like such a bastard for making her so upset. "I'm sorry, so sorry."

She sobbed in his arms as though her heart was breaking, and if hers was anything like his, then it was rupturing, splintering. Her fists gripped his shirt, pulling it tight, pinching his skin, but he didn't care. Nothing mattered except she was in his arms where she belonged.

For several minutes they stayed that way until a cramp in his calf muscle forced Patrick to swivel sideways, bringing Fleur with him to sit with his back against the sofa and her on his lap. He kissed her hair, her cheeks, her eyes and she shuddered in his embrace. "We're a fine pair, aren't we?" He chuckled. He was getting soft.

Fleur snuggled deeper into his arms—if that was possible. "What are we to do?"

"I don't know, sweetheart." The whole situation was a diabolical mess, but he couldn't walk away from her now that his anger had gone. It might have been easier to do in a rage, but having her in his arms was heaven on earth and nothing could part him from her at this moment.

She hiccupped on a lingering sob, her voice wavering. "I love you."

Resting his head against hers, he smiled. Emotion still tight in his throat made his voice husky. "And I love you."

"Really?" Hope lightened her eyes.

"Seems that way." He winked and kissed the tip of her nose. "I don't think it's good for me to love you, but I do all the same."

Chuckling, she stroked his cheek. "Well you're like sticky donuts, bad for me but irresistible."

He laughed. "I don't think I've ever been compared to a donut before."

"Well, there are worse things."

"I guess so." He squeezed her gently. The joy of having her near him was enough for now. Whatever happened tomorrow or the next day, happened. They'd deal with it somehow.

"Will you stay the night?"

Patrick nuzzled her ear. Loving her, wanting her, needing her in his life. "Try and stop me, beautiful," he whispered.

Chapter Eleven

Fleur rifled through the top drawer of the tallboy in the bedroom looking for her lease agreement. “Where the hell is it?” She frowned and scratched her forehead, gazing around the room as if hoping it would suddenly jump up and dance the rumba in front of her.

The only place she kept important documents was in this drawer.

Taking a deep breath she began again.

“Fleur?”

She glanced out the bedroom door. “In here, Rachel.”

Rachel, clad in jeans and a yellow T-shirt, entered but instead of sitting on the bed as she’d normally do, hovered by the door not saying anything.

Distracted, Fleur stopped rummaging and looked at her friend’s pale face. “What’s the matter? Is Courtney sick again?”

“No. No nothing like that.” Rachel smiled nervously.

“What then?”

“Well...” Rachel tilted her head. “Um... How did it go with Patrick? I saw him arrive yesterday and that’s why I didn’t come over.”

Fleur rested her hand on the drawer edge and sighed. Last night they'd made love like it would be their last time, which was silly really, as they both agreed they couldn't give the other up, so they'd be bound to make love again soon—like tonight. "We talked. We argued. We cried."

Rachel walked over and gave her a hug. "Must have been awful."

"It was..." She shrugged. Their future was uncertain—that was the only sure thing she knew. "Anyway, we're going to take it one day at a time."

"Good idea." Rachel stepped to the window and gazed down at the street below.

Puzzled, Fleur watched her. Something was on her mind. "What is it, Rachel?"

"Well..."

Fleur closed the drawer, giving her full attention.

Rachel's smiled wavered as she left the window and sat on the bed. "I've been talking with Mum and we sort of came up with an idea..."

"Oh?"

Clasping her hands together, Rachel seemed to have lost the art of breathing.

Frowning at her friend's obvious discomfort, Fleur crossed to sit beside her. "You look worried."

"No, I'm not. It's just difficult."

"What is?"

Rachel took a deep breath. "Look, I'll understand if you say no."

"About what?"

"Mum and I thought... We decided that it would be nice if, with your permission of course—"

Fleur laughed. "For heaven's sake, Rachel, spit it out."

"We want to take over the shop," she blurted.

Amazed, Fleur stared at her. How incredible. She never would have guessed it was that. "Really? You really want the shop?"

Rachel nodded, a blush creeping up her cheeks. "Only if it's okay with you."

"It never crossed my mind you'd want to." Fleur rose, her mind whirling. Her shop. Rachel wanted her shop. She didn't know what to think.

"Listen, Fleur, it's okay if you don't want us to. I'd understand."

"No, it isn't that. I'm just shocked, that's all."

"Do you hate the idea?" Rachel rose too and stood facing her, concern etching her features.

"No..." Fleur shook her head slowly. "No, I don't hate the idea at all." Abruptly the suggestion took hold and grew into a likable prospect. She smiled. "Actually, I like the idea of someone, of *you* taking the shop over."

"Truly?"

"Absolutely." It felt like a huge weight had been lifted off her shoulders. That her little shop would be cared for and loved filled her with pleasure.

Rachel let out a long breath. "I'm so glad. I was really worried you'd hate the whole thing. We'll give you money for the stock and everything. How much will you want?"

Taken aback, Fleur shook her head. "No, I don't want your money." It appalled her to even think of taking Rachel's money.

She knew how much she struggled on her sole mother's pension.

"I must pay you something. You bought all that stock and furniture."

"There's hardly any stock actually and it's all secondhand. The books were from boot sales." She thought quickly. "Look, to break my lease I'd have to pay the landlord the rent money owing up to the end of September or October. I can't remember which." She waved her hand dismissively. "Anyway, if you take on the lease then you'll be saving me money. So, we can call that the payment for the stock. Okay?"

"No, Fleur. That's not right. It's not enough for you."

"Rachel, I don't want your money. I will never take it. I have a business and money at home. I'm fine, honestly."

"Are you positive?"

"Very."

"Okay, thanks so much. It's wonderful of you."

"Think nothing of it." Fleur smiled and gave her a hug. "But how will you run it with Courtney?"

"That's where Mum comes into it. She wants to be my partner."

"You're kidding." Fleur grinned.

"Nope. She enjoyed looking after it when Courtney was in hospital. She always wanted a shop but Dad would never let her, but now he's retired, he's happy for her to do as she pleases."

"So, you'll move from your flat over to this one?"

Rachel's face glowed with excitement. "No. I'll stay in my flat and Mum and Dad will move in here."

"No! Really? They want to move into this tiny flat?"

Rachel nodded, laughing. "Dad hates gardening. He much prefers watching sports on TV. So every summer they argue over the state of the garden. Dad doesn't mind moving into this flat because it gets him out of mowing the lawn in summer, plus he's closer to the shops when he needs to go to the bookies or to buy his paper."

"I don't believe it." Fleur linked her arm through Rachel's and they went into the kitchen. "Let's have a coffee to celebrate. Shame I don't have anything stronger."

"I can't get too excited just yet. We still need to speak with the landlord."

Fleur stuck the kettle under the tap and added water. "I'm seeing him soon. We can talk to him together if you want."

"Yes, please. Safety in numbers and all that." Rachel laughed and then looked worried again. "Do you think he'd say no?"

"I shouldn't see why he would." Fleur switched the kettle on and got the cups out. "All it requires is to swap the lease over into your name."

"Yes. There's that and then the changing over of the shop equipment into my name, too. Also I'll have to find out about getting a wholesaler's card." She tucked her dark hair behind her ear. "There's so much to do and consider."

"What about winter though? How will you keep it going over winter when the tourist numbers drop?"

"We discussed that and came up with the idea of hot food to sell. Mum makes excellent soups and curries. We thought if we promote the shop well enough we should be able to survive through until the summer. If necessary I'll get a part-time job to tide us over."

Fleur smiled. "Sounds like you've got it all worked out."

"Well, it's a great opportunity for me and Courtney and for Mum, too."

"I'm so pleased. It'll be comforting to know the shop will live on after I've left Whitby."

Rachel nodded with tears in her eyes. "And it'll always give me a reminder of your time here and the great friend you've become to me." She sniffed and laughed at her own emotions. "I promised myself I wouldn't cry about you leaving. Promise we'll not lose touch."

Fleur reached for her hand and gripped it. "I promise."

The announcer's voice crackled over the airport's intercom, informing the crowds that the flight departing for Paris was now ready for boarding.

Fleur concentrated on her breathing. In out. In out. Beside her, Patrick was blatantly chatting up the café's waitress, who took their order. After giving the goggling waitress a gorgeous smile, he turned back to Fleur.

"You okay?"

She nodded. His pretend flirting didn't bother her. She knew he was doing it to wind her up and keep the atmosphere light. This dreadful day had to be endured and laughter was better than tears. They would come soon enough. "Did she give you her number?"

"No, damn it."

"Better luck next time."

He grinned and turned away, but as he did so he took her hand and held it tight. The warmth and strength she felt from him helped.

They focused on their surroundings, pushing their joint misery away to the back of their minds. Thankfully, there was always something to look at in airports. People of every nationality walked by.

Fleur played her favorite airport-waiting-lounge game. She liked to imagine or guess each person's destination or where they were returning from.

A man passed by wearing a loud, colorful shirt with sandals on his feet. Spain.

Next was a group of young men, lads really, and all worse for wear with awful sunburned red faces and bleary eyes. Ibiza.

A short, plump, elderly woman completely dressed in black sat across from them surrounded by numerous members of her family. Italy.

A man in a tailored suit with a scowling face, who checked his watch every two minutes. New York.

"Fleur?"

Blinking, she looked at Patrick. His wry smile and tilt of head alerted her that their cappuccinos and sandwiches had arrived.

"Sorry." She sat forward. It was a good game for it had given her numerous minutes of not thinking about leaving Patrick. Again, now reminded, her heart squeezed painfully. How could she do it? She was putting everything before him and their relationship. Insane. Gazing at him, she studied his rugged handsomeness, his lovely blue eyes, hair too long still, the way his wide shoulders filled out his leather jacket. He was a walking sex advertisement.

And I'm leaving him.

The salad sandwich stuck in her throat. She had to get through this day. It would be much easier after today. They ate halfheartedly, not concerned with the food, simply not hungry. Patrick soon pushed his plate away and Fleur did the same. Instinctively they held hands and smiled.

"Now, you have all my details written down, email address, fax number, everything?" He rubbed his thumb over her knuckles. "Don't keep all the information in your mobile in case you lose it."

"It's okay, darling. I have it all in my diary, too."

"Okay." He glanced away and she knew his pain, felt it as well.

All too soon the airport announcer told passengers that Qantas flight 02 was ready to board.

Her flight.

The time had come. She couldn't feel her legs.

"That's you." Patrick stood and helped Fleur gather her things. She grabbed her handbag and he picked up the hand luggage. Without speaking, they walked to the boarding lounge. Already a queue waited their turn to walk through the metal detectors. Holding back from the crowd, Fleur gripped Patrick's hand tighter. She sucked in deep breaths to steady the urge to howl like a baby.

"I love you," Patrick whispered, his voice gravelly with emotion.

She threw herself into his arms and he lifted her up off the floor, squeezing her so hard she thought he'd break a rib, but she didn't care, not for a minute.

"I love you." She cried into his neck, her fingers curling into his jacket. "I'll contact you every day, I promise."

"You'd better do." He kissed her passionately, holding her length against him.

Slowly they drew apart. Fleur couldn't care less about the state she was in. No doubt her mascara had run, but Patrick gazed lovingly at her and made her feel beautiful. "It won't be long until Christmas, and then you'll be with me."

He grinned, blinking away his own tears. "Four weeks in the sun. I can't wait."

"We'll have a great time. There's so much I want to show you."

"Yes, but I want to spend the first week in bed."

"Then you'd better make it five weeks." She laughed and then kissed him hard, stamping her print on him forever.

The queue had all but disappeared and panic flooded her, as she knew she must go. Think of Christmas, think of Christmas...

"Ring me the minute you land in Sydney, no matter what time." Patrick pulled her to him once more and kissed the side of her head. "I want to know that you've arrived safely."

"I will." She stepped away and only their hands touched. Letting go of one of his hands, she reached down and picked up her small luggage bag all the while not taking her eyes off him.

A tear slowly tracked its way down Patrick's cheek and at the sight of it, a sob broke from Fleur. Men crying always killed her, but this was even worse, this was Patrick crying for her, for their wretched future that they couldn't plan for.

"I love you," she whispered.

"I can't bear this, Fleur. I have to go." Patrick's voice caught. He dropped her other hand and strode away.

She no longer had a heart. It had exploded and the pieces were floating around her body, never to be put together again because she had a strange feeling that she'd never see him again.

She stood at the boarding gate and watched him walk away with his head high and shoulders straight. Typical. The man must hide his grief, pretend it wasn't there. Whereas a woman would stumble, crawl, scream at the world and cry. Like she was doing. Crying an ocean. They could send her to the Gulf, after a while there she'd have turned the desert into a rainforest. Could you die from over crying?

She sniffed and gulped. So, that was it. All over red rover.

On automatic pilot she handed her boarding pass to the stewardess and went through the detector. The attendants smiled in sympathy at her ravaged face. She hated them. Collecting her things again from the conveyer, she paused and couldn't help but look back over her shoulder. He hadn't come back. Of course he wouldn't. Silly woman, what did she expect? What would it achieve? They'd talked until they were blue in the face about what they should, could, would do, but in the end it'd all come down to her catching a plane and flying home.

A black pit of despair swallowed her whole.

In a void, she walked into the plane and was shown her seat and had her luggage stowed away by a neatly polished and smiling stewardess, who didn't seem to have a care in the world. Bitch. Didn't she know that Fleur Stanthorpe was dying inside? It was world news, devastating news. For the first time in her independent life, Fleur Stanthorpe was finding out how it felt to truly love another. She couldn't breathe. Oh, great she was going to have a heart attack on the plane.

Stumbling a little, she fell into her seat. She was all fingers and thumbs, but managed to click on her seat belt before glancing out the tiny window, not that she saw much, tears blurred her vision like a misty veil. She let the tears fall, not caring to wipe them away. Stuff it. Stuff it all.

Fleur was jolted out of her misery as the plane's doors were jammed into place. Passengers' chatter dimmed. The engines grew louder and signs flashed to fasten seat belts. She frowned and stared around. They were pulling away from the airport building. Where was everyone? The two seats beside her remained empty. Empty?

A young, fresh-faced steward paused in the aisle and smiled. "Got your seat belt fastened? Yes, good."

She swallowed—smiling was impossible. "I think the people sitting here must be in the loos."

"Oh, no." He smiled like a saint. "Those seats are empty all the way to Sydney. Aren't you the lucky one?" He went on with his checking as the plane taxied to the runway and she stared at the seats like they were full of vipers. Just this once a crazy neighbor would have been a distraction. She was cursed.

Covering her face with her hands, she cried silently while the plane gathered speed and lifted them off the ground. Away from England. Away from Patrick.

Chapter Twelve

Geoffrey Fitz John approached the golden light. Stiffly, and trying not to make too much noise with his armor, he bent down on one knee before the table. Within the shadows, a priest's voice droned, but Geoffrey was too concerned about the coming battle to take any interest in the Latin verses.

He wasn't a praying man, but then...

His hands shook. Sweat beaded on his upper lip. He concentrated on the candles. The flames wavered slightly as the door opened and another knight entered and noisily knelt in prayer beside him. Frowning, Geoffrey stared harder at the shimmering glow, willing for inner peace. To lead his men into battle he needed a clear head—a clear soul. He should pray for victory. Yet, within the flickering circle of light, all he thought of was Rosalind.

Rosalind the Fair. His wife. His heart.

They had a good life and he must protect it. Protect them. But who knew what waited on the other side of a battle. His family would be taken cared of if...

No. He mustn't think the worst. The candle flames spluttered, then straightened once more. He steadied his breathing, allowing the peace of the room to flow over him.

"It is time, Sir," a voice spoke from behind.

Geoffrey nodded and rose. Rosalind had suggested he come here, away from the yard full of bustling soldiers, to help him prepare. This was sanctuary and she'd wanted him to know of its power. She had been right, as always. With ease of heart he turned to his man. "I am ready."

After a last glance at the table, he walked towards the light of the open doorway. He'd be back.

The loud splash gave Fleur little warning before a spray of water rained down on her where she sat reclining by the pool. "What the hell."

Charlie emerged from the water at the other end of the pool and laughed. "Hello, Sis."

"Bloody hell, Charlie, grow up!" Furious, Fleur tried to wipe off most of the moisture from her book. Damn. The one time she'd been really absorbed, really enjoying being out of her world and her stupid brother ruined it.

Charlie swam to her side of the pool and popped his head up over the edge, his normal sandy blond hair plastered darkly to his head. "Sorry."

"No, you're not." She didn't even look at him as she continued to wipe off the water, this time from her legs, which combined with the generous helping of sun-cream now became an oily mess. "Every time I'm near the pool you have to behave like a five-year-old again."

"Oh, stop overreacting." He grinned.

She glared at him. "I've come here for a few hours of peace, Charlie. Can I have that please?"

He backstroked away a few paces, spouting water into the air like a whale. "What's wrong with your place?"

Fleur threw her beach towel onto the next sun chair. "The smell of paint is still too strong. Mum said I could spend the day here while it aired out a bit more."

"Coming in for a swim?"

"No." She shook her head. The weather was hot for November. Summer had arrived early and the water looked inviting but she'd been eager to finish the historical novel she'd bought a few days ago. A novel that helped ease her mind from always straying to thinking about Patrick. "I wanted to read for a while."

"I'm not stopping you." He swam back to her and grinned his cheeky boy smile that made him popular with all the girls—that and his dark tan and good physique. Charlie was a bloke's bloke. All football, fast cars and joking around. He surprised everyone when he announced his engagement to Susannah. Fleur still couldn't believe her great big silly brother would be married next month.

Gathering up her things, Fleur stood and walked to the gate.

"Hey, Fleur. You don't have to go." Charlie laughed. "I'll be good."

"That'll make a change, Charles." Her sarcasm just made him laugh, which annoyed her further. Leaving the pool area, she walked across the lush well-trimmed lawn, her father's pet project, and towards the house. Damn Charlie! It'd been so nice to just sit and escape her mind for a short time. To have an hour or so without dwelling on Patrick.

Her stomach clenched, as it always did whenever she thought of Patrick. How she missed him. Ached for him. The last she'd heard from him was two days ago when he phoned her late at night. He now spent a lot of his time going between Whitby and Manchester. The new restaurant had opened last month, and with it being a bigger venue and being in a more populated area, it was busier, more stressful. She understood this and knew how difficult it was to overcome time differences and running a successful business. Yet, they had to make or find time. It was paramount to their relationship's survival.

"Hi, Fleur."

She looked up and smiled at Susannah who was walking out of the back door with towels and a magazine under her arm. "Hello there. Did you just arrive?"

"Yes. A few minutes ago, was just talking to your mum." Susannah smiled, her sunglasses hiding her soft blue eyes that were always warm and friendly. Fleur liked the idea of her becoming an addition to the family. She'd never had a sister before so a sister-in-law was the next best thing, especially if it meant having someone as nice as Susannah.

Fleur gave her a kiss on the cheek. "Try and drown Charlie for me, will you?" She laughed.

"Oh no, what's he done now?" Susannah rolled her eyes. "I told him not to disturb you."

"Well it didn't work. You need to bring him under control more."

"I'll do my best, but it's a work in progress."

Laughing, Fleur went inside and took off her sunglasses. The coolness of the kitchen made her shiver after the heat of outside. Opening the fridge, she took out a jug of orange juice and placed it on the bench. She put her book in her bag with a sense of longing. The story had engrossed her. Perhaps she should go back to the apartment and finish it, but the thought of the lingering paint smells put her off. She'd wait until tonight when she could run a nice bubble bath and finish reading the book then. It made her grin at the thought of how many relaxing baths she'd taken since returning from England. Ironic.

"Do you want a cup of coffee, darling?" her mother asked, coming into the kitchen with an armload of dirty clothes for washing.

"No thanks, Mum."

"Did Charlie disturb you?" Val frowned. "I warned him to leave you alone. You've had a busy week this week."

Fleur smiled and reached for a glass from the top cupboard. "When has warning Charlie ever stopped him from doing something idiotic?"

"Yes, I know." Her mother disappeared into the adjoining laundry room, and Fleur poured out the juice and then took it out onto the patio. The air was rich with scent from the roses and lavender in the garden. Lavender... Making love with Patrick...

She pushed the image from her mind. Not now.

Large trees hid half the pool from view, but she smiled as Susannah's shouts and cries could be heard, as no doubt Charlie was doing his best to torment her. His favorite game was playing Jaws. He was such a big kid.

"Those two." Her mother joined her, shaking her head and smiling in fondness. "I can't believe we'll be having a wedding here next month."

"I can't believe Charlie managed to commit to one woman, you know how he was as a teenager. He had a different girl every Friday night."

Val chuckled. "That's boys for you. But he's grown up, matured at last." She laughed louder. "Who'd have predicted that Charlie suggested getting married to Susannah first? I'd thought he'd run a mile at the mere thought, but Susannah tells me he's been hinting at it for a while before he popped the question."

Fleur remained silent, emotion suddenly blocking her throat. She wanted marriage, too. She wanted marriage and children. How was she going to manage it? Patrick seemed further away than just physical distance. He had people depending on him, family, commitments as she had. His whole life was over there and hers was here. With each passing day it seemed impossible that they'd work this out. Emails and phone calls were a poor substitute. She had a hideous premonition that they would simply drift apart and look back on their time together as a holiday fling. Just like Angela predicted. A stab of pain hit her.

"They are happy, aren't they, Fleur? I mean, they look like they'll make a go of their marriage."

Nodding, she patted her mum's arm and tried not to think of her problems and instead focused on Charlie's wedding. "They'll be fine, Mum. Susannah is good for Charlie. It's a good match."

Val nodded. "Yes, you're right." She turned away from the splashing lovers and looked directly at Fleur. "But what about you? You don't look happy. Is everything all right at the bakery?"

"It's so hot." Fleur turned and went inside with Val following close behind.

"Fleur?"

Sitting on the barstool at the kitchen bench, Fleur drained her glass and refilled it. Trust her mother to think of the bakery before her relationship. As far as her mother was concerned, all that happened in England no longer mattered. Fleur sighed and struggled to forgive her mum's shortcomings. "Yes, the bakery is going well. Better than I could hope for. It just about runs itself. The staff, as you know, are very good and have been doing it long enough without the need for me to hover over them."

"And you enjoy serving in the shop? I mean you don't need to, there's enough girls already employed to do it."

"Serving gives me something to do." And keeps me occupied.

"Why don't you take another baker's course?"

"The shop doesn't need another baker, Mum." It doesn't need me at all.

Val's smile was tight. "And the renovations at the apartment? How are they going?"

"Nearly finished. Now that the painting has been done, I'll get the carpets ripped up and new ones laid or I might even polish the floorboards if they look good enough." She gazed down at the drink.

She'd have gone mad without the shop and apartment to keep her busy. Working in the shop every day behind the counter and then decorating and updating the apartment in the evenings kept the lonely hours at bay. If she tried hard enough whole minutes could go by without her thinking of Patrick.

"Then why the long face?" Val fetched a glass for herself and poured out some juice. A coolness entered her eyes. "You have so much to be grateful for, Fleur, yet you barely smile."

"Need you ask?"

"I don't understand you sometimes."

"Why?" Fleur glared at her. "Why am I so hard to understand?"

"Because you always make things difficult. Only you would insist on spending the summer in England when you had a family here who wanted to spend time with you after you became well."

"I'm not getting into this again, Mum. We sorted all this out after Uncle Harry's funeral."

"Did we? It doesn't feel like you took any of it in." Val snorted. "You said that you'd come home and settle down and be happy so that your father and I wouldn't worry ourselves into an early grave over you."

"I am happy," she lied.

"Are you?" Her mother tossed her head, red spots of anger coloring her cheeks. "You may have come home, Fleur, but you certainly aren't happy and because of that we're all paying the price."

"How are you paying the price?" Fleur wanted to scream in frustration. Her mother always did this, always made her feel in the wrong.

"We have to put up with you being miserable and moping around as though your world has come to an end. Heavens, Fleur. You've survived cancer and been given a second chance. Why aren't you living?"

White-hot anger and pain shot through her. "I can't live as I want to because the man I love is on the other side of the world. But do you care?" Fleur folded her arms across her chest in disgust and disappointment. "No, you don't give a fig about that."

Her mother sighed deeply. She looked tired. "That's not true."

"Don't lie to me, Mum. You hate the fact Patrick exists."

"I don't hate him. I'm just disappointed you had to fall in love with someone so unsuitable."

Fleur felt the anger leave her and despair replace it. "He's not unsuitable."

"He lives in another country."

Her mother's refusal to include Patrick in her life, and despite the fact he was thousands of miles away, didn't stop her from loving him, missing him. She tried to see it from her mother's point of view. Patrick was a threat to her family life, for while he lingered around, Fleur could suddenly disappear again, and try as she might, Fleur couldn't totally convince her that she wasn't about to hop on the next plane to England because it was exactly what she wanted to do. Only she couldn't and the reason for that was...she was too frightened of her reception.

Too many days had gone by now, it was just like the first time she and Patrick were apart. Time played funny tricks on relationships. What was once secure and blissful abruptly became awkward and uncertain.

"Have you heard from him lately?"

"Yes. He rang a couple of days ago." She ran her finger around the rim of the glass. "He's been so busy, like I have. It's hard."

"Impossible I'd say." Val turned away to stare out the kitchen window.

"I love him, Mum."

"I know."

Fleur looked at the rigid profile and sighed. "I want what Charlie and Susannah have. Is that too much to ask?"

"No, of course not." Val glanced at her. "I want you to be happy too, but this isn't making you content and we all know it. I wake up every day wondering if you're going to tell us you're going back to England. I dread every time I see you in case you tell me you're going away again. I'm tired of worrying over you. You're nearly thirty years old and we've never stopped worrying over you. We'd like a break, please. I think we've earned it."

Fleur bowed her head, guilt filling her. Her mother knew her so well. Many times in the last months all she wanted to do was go to England and throw herself into Patrick's arms, and it was only the thought of hurting her family that stopped her. "I can't turn off my feelings, Mum."

"What about his feelings? How do you know he really loves you?"

"He told me." *I can't stand this.* "I know he loves me."

"Let us hope he truly does and that he's worth all this upset. Is he still coming out at Christmas?"

"Yes, I think so. We didn't mention it in our last conversation."

"I would've thought it was something constantly talked about. Isn't he excited to be coming here?

"I'm sure he is. But we talked of other things. He mentioned he'd seen Rachel in the supermarket and stuff like that." Fleur frowned, remembering that last phone call. Patrick had been tired, distracted and she had been on tenterhooks waiting for him to reaffirm his love for her. Was she becoming neurotic? She'd never been one of those women who needed continuous confirmation from their partners that they were loved. She dismissed the thought. It was the distance, that's all.

Her mother opened up the dishwasher and started unloading the clean plates. "I just don't want him to hurt you, Fleur. With the wedding coming up and Christmas I want it to be a lovely time for us all. We've been through enough with your cancer and then Harry's death. Your father has had a stressful time at work and then he lost his brother. You know how close they were. He's having trouble accepting it. Harry was the only family he had in Australia."

"Yes, I know. And Christmas will be great, I promise."

"Not if Patrick doesn't show up it won't be." Plates were dumped not so gently onto the bench. "If he puts off coming here, you'll be upset and that'll make everything difficult."

"Why wouldn't he come?" Fleur stood, once again annoyed at her mother's lack of trust in Patrick—someone she didn't even know. "Besides, even if he didn't come out here, I'd still be pleased for Charlie and I wouldn't ruin their day. I'm not a child." Grabbing her things, she stuffed them into the large canvas bag she always used to take to the beach or pool. She had to get away from her mother. She couldn't cope with all this negativity; she could do that well enough on her own.

Val straightened. "Don't get all heated on me. I'm merely saying, that's all."

"Well don't." Fleur pushed her feet into her sandals. "I don't need you to do this, Mum. I don't need you to make me feel sick to my stomach at the thought of never seeing Patrick again, okay?"

"Hey, what's this?" Charlie opened the back screen door.

"Nothing." Fleur went up and kissed his cheek. "I'm going. I'll see you soon."

"Wait." Charlie held her arm and looked at their mother before back at Fleur. "Why are you upset?"

"I'm not." Fleur forced a smile past the misery choking her. "I've got paperwork to do and stuff."

Val closed the dishwasher. "Fleur, sit down and we'll have a cup of coffee. Your dad will be home from golf soon."

"No, thanks. I've got to go."

"Listen, I'm sorry if I upset you. You know I didn't mean to."

"Didn't you?" Fleur shrugged. "It doesn't matter, Mum, because you could be right. By the time Christmas comes

Patrick might not think our relationship is worth pursuing. I'll see you later." Fleur left before her mother could answer.

She ran lightly out the front door and to her car with tears hovering on her eyelashes. Once in the car, she searched her bag for her mobile and hurriedly pressed speed dial for Patrick's number.

The phone rang for ages, and Fleur didn't have the presence of mind to work out what time it was in England, but nor did she care.

"Hello?" Patrick's voice sounded sleepy, rough.

"It's me," Fleur whispered.

"Fleur? What time is it?"

"Um, I don't know." She looked at her watch but couldn't make out the time with her tears blurring her vision, never mind working out what it was in England. "I'm sorry I woke you."

"Is something wrong?"

"No. Yes."

"What?"

"I miss you." Her voice broke on a sob and, horrified that he'd know she was crying, she quickly stuck her hand over her mouth.

"I miss you, too, sweetheart."

She nodded, feeling better. "This is hard."

"I know. I'm sorry."

"It was wrong of me to wake you. I was having a weak moment."

"That's okay. It's not every morning at...five past four...that I get woken up by a beautiful woman."

"Good. I'd hate to think you were." She smiled, hearing the warmth in his voice. It only added to her ache, but at least it reassured her somewhat. "Go back to bed."

"I'm in bed."

The image of him lying naked tangled in amongst the sheets made her hot and needy. "I meant go back to sleep."

"Okay. I'll ring you tonight my time. We might be able to participate in a little bit of phone sex. What do you think?"

She laughed and wiped away her tears. "Sounds good. Phone sex while I'm eating breakfast is always a good start to the day."

"It'll be all right, sweetheart. I promise."

Her laughter died. "I hope so. Apparently I'm making everyone's life terrible here."

Chapter Thirteen

Click.

With one hit of a button the computer screen went blank. Fleur stared at it and tried not to feel disappointed, but she was. She gently touched the screen where moments ago his face had appeared. Every time she finished talking to Patrick on the webcam she had a period of downtime. Seeing his face on the screen once a week, plus their phone calls and text messages, was all she had to keep their relationship alive. And now he'd just informed her that he was going to Ireland for a week to visit his parents and attend a cousin's wedding. For a week all she'd have was the odd phone call and text message. It wasn't enough.

Sighing, she left the desk and stretched. Outside the window, the hot December day burned the good people of Camden. She looked around the comfortable, air-conditioned apartment. The renovations were complete and the apartment sparkled like a diamond. The polished floorboards, fresh paint, new solid wooden furniture, rugs, prints on the walls and vases full of either dry or fresh flowers looked amazing. She was so proud of it, as it had all been chosen by her, for this her first real home of her own. The project had kept her busy too, and lessened the time she spent worrying about Patrick losing interest in her. Yes, the apartment renovations were a godsend really, but it was finished and she had nothing left to do.

On the coffee table, between the new white leather sofas, sat a stack of magazines and a few brochures on what to do in New South Wales. She'd collected them to help her construct an itinerary for Patrick's stay. However, Patrick hadn't seemed too interested when she mentioned it just now. He was tired, she knew that, and it was late at night for him when they spoke, but still, a little more enthusiasm wouldn't hurt.

The door buzzer rang and she crossed over to answer it. Opening the door, her eyes widened as Charlie stood filling the doorway in his dusty work clothes of old jeans and T-shirt, baseball cap and boots.

"Hello. Why are you here and not at work?"

"I had a few things I needed to do and being the boss of Stanthorpe Constructions, I made an executive decision to have lunch early." Charlie grinned and followed her into the kitchen.

"It's good being the boss."

"Absolutely. I've got a heap of work on, but most of the jobs won't be finished until after the Christmas break. I've just come from a job at Campbelltown and I've got to check on some laborers working on a new house in Cobbitty." He stopped and gazed around appreciatively. "You've done an excellent job with the décor, Fleur."

"Thank you." She smiled. "Want a drink?"

"Got something cold? It's hot enough out there to fry an egg."

She opened the fridge. "I've a few cans of Coke?"

"That'll do, ta." He leaned against the kitchen bench. "Why aren't you in the shop?"

Fleur shrugged. “There’s enough girls serving without me there.” She handed him a can.

“You need to do something. You’ve got too much time on your hands.”

“I know. It drives me crazy.”

Charlie peered at her, the can left unopened in his hands. “You’ve got that look about you.”

“What look?” She frowned and walked around the bench and into the living room. The open-plan design made it easy to talk to people from both rooms.

Not following her, Charlie simply turned and rested his elbows on the Formica bench top, his expression worried. “You look restless and when you get restless you end up disappearing on us for a while. What’s wrong?”

Fleur straightened the already tidy pile of magazines. “I miss Patrick.”

“He’ll be here soon.”

“Will he?” She moved to the bookshelves and fussed with some books not standing upright.

“You think he won’t?”

“I don’t know.”

“What did he say when you last spoke?”

“I was speaking to him via the webcam just before you arrived. He seems...oh, I don’t know...distant.”

“Are you sure he just wasn’t tired or got the flu or something?”

Fleur shook her head and stepped to the dining table situated between the kitchen and living room. She ran her finger along the polished wood and inspected it for dust. Perhaps Patrick was only tired, but deep down she doubted it.

The distance, the time apart, was starting to show. Minuscule cracks were beginning to appear in their relationship.

Charlie came to her side and placed his hand on her shoulder. "You want to go back to England, don't you?"

She swallowed and reached over to fondle the blue irises in the vase on the middle of the table. "Not England exactly, just Patrick. I want to be with him. I don't care where that is, England, Ireland, Australia as long as we're together that's all I want."

He sighed, flicked back the opening of his can and took a long drink. "I've never seen you like this over a guy before. You've always been a love-em and leave-em type."

Chuckling, Fleur folded her arms. "Yes well, now I know why I was. It was to prevent feeling like this." She went and sat on the sofa. "I hate it, Charlie. I hate being so helpless and insecure."

Slouching down beside her, he grinned. "I'm so thankful I'm getting married. Dating sucks."

"Yes it does. Big time."

"Christmas isn't far away. Two more weeks. Just think about spending your first Christmas with him."

"Will he be here though? I have a feeling he won't come. He leaves for Ireland tomorrow for a week, then he has Christmas parties to attend before he jets out here on the twenty-third."

"Twenty-third?" Charlie frowned. "I thought he was coming out earlier, like the end of this week?"

"His plans changed last week. He forgot about some cousin's wedding in Ireland and other stuff. The new restaurant in Manchester is doing brilliantly, much more than Patrick expected."

"You must be disappointed he's been delayed then?"

"Of course. Sometimes I wonder if he's just looking for excuses not to come."

"Does that sound like something he'd do? If it is, then you're better off without him honestly."

She gave him a wry smile. "Tell that to my heart. Besides, he's not like that. Patrick has always been honest with me. If he wanted to end it then he would tell me, I'm sure." Frowning, she realized what she said was true. He *would* tell her. So why was she being so stupid and worrying that their relationship was about to end? If Patrick wanted it to finish it would be by now.

Suddenly, it was like a light bulb being switched on inside her head.

How stupid was she? She'd been tormenting herself over something that didn't exist.

Relaxing slightly, she breathed easier and felt better. She had to take heart of her own reasoning. She knew Patrick.

Fleur gazed down at her fingernails that she'd freshly painted that morning—again to give her something to do. "I think that if Patrick doesn't come out here I might go over there and see him."

"What about my wedding?" Charlie stared at her in panic. "You can't miss my wedding."

"It's okay, I'll go after the wedding."

"Why go at all? If the guy doesn't come here as planned and fills you with lame excuses as to why he didn't, then ditch him. There's loads of other guys out there, who live in *this* country."

Fleur shook her head. Thinking about it more she felt she understood what was happening. At last. "No. Patrick leads a full life. Actually, his life is much busier than I ever realized. He always made time for me without letting me know just what it took for him to do it. Until this moment I never really understood that."

"Mum and Dad will have a fit if you emigrate to England."

She looked at him from under her lashes, knowing the hurt she would give her family. "I have to be with him, Charlie. He's the one."

Charlie closed his eyes momentarily. "Don't go, Fleur. You've got a life here."

"What is my life without him in it? It's an empty shell."

"Only because you're bored, the shop isn't enough for you. Do something else, take a course in...reflexology or tattooing or bungee jumping."

She laughed and kissed his cheek. "Yes, I am bored, but that's because I'm not settled."

His look was incredulous. "You have a lovely place to live, money and family. To me that's being settled."

"I need Patrick."

Charlie went to speak but his mobile rang. He looked at the caller's number and then switched it off. "Bugger. Look, I have to go. I've left the boys on a job site and we want to get it finished before the end of next week."

"Of course. Thanks for stopping by." Fleur walked with him to the door and he handed her his empty can.

He paused in the doorway. "You won't make any hasty decisions, will you? Because the thought of you living permanently in England just kills me."

She rubbed her hand up and down his muscular arm. How she loved him—all six-foot-three of him. "You'll be busy with your own life."

"You are a part of that life." He scratched his head, frowning. "Look, I wasn't meant to mention this and Susannah will cut my thingy off for doing so but, well...I don't want you to go because you'll miss seeing my baby."

"What?" Fleur scowled in puzzlement. "What do you mean?"

Charlie looked sheepish. "Susannah is pregnant."

"Oh my God!" Fleur flung herself into his arms. "This is brilliant news."

Charlie grinned as though he'd done something so amazing, something that no one else had ever done. "I know. I'm stoked."

Fleur felt the urge to cry at such glorious news. "Oh, Charlie. I can't believe it. When's the baby due?"

"End of May. But don't tell anyone yet. We're going to announce it at the wedding."

"Everyone's going to be excited. Mum will simply die of happiness."

A serious look came into his eyes. "That's why you can't live in England, Fleur. Your family is here."

Fleur paced the floor of her apartment. For the week Patrick was in Ireland, he text messaged her every day, but only called once from his mobile, which she accepted without any qualms as she knew it would have been difficult for him to always get in contact with her while he was there. Apparently every day for that week he'd been busy with family and friends.

However, since his arrival back in England, she'd received nothing. No phone calls, no texts, no emails. She didn't even know if he was leaving on the twenty-third, which was tomorrow.

He wasn't answering his mobile or the phone in his flat.

Frustrated and angry, she looked at the clock on the wall and worked out that it was nine o'clock at night in England. Picking up her phone, she dialed his flat again. The phone rang out. She tried his mobile. Same thing happened. The phone rang out and then went to his voice mail.

She swore badly and wiped her hand over her eyes. This was a nightmare. Then a sickened thought hit her. What if he was ill or had an accident? Would his parents think to contact her? Could they contact her? Did they know her last name?

Oh my God!

"Take a deep breath, Fleur," she whispered. "Don't get carried away and all dramatic." She looked down at her mobile in her hand and willed it to ring. "Please, please, please!"

It didn't.

"Right. Let's think about this rationally." She started her pacing once more, biting her lip while thinking of what to do next. She could ring information and find out all the people called Donnelly in... Damn. What was the village called where Patrick came from? Bally... Ballysomething.

She stared at the floor, frowning hard, trying to remember. How could she forget such information? Her mind went totally blank.

"This is not good." Fleur threw her head back and gazed at the ceiling but the name wouldn't come. "Okay, think of something else."

The phone suddenly rang and Fleur nearly broke her leg dashing around the coffee table to answer it. "Hello? Patrick?"

"No, it's Mum."

"Oh, hi, Mum." Fleur sighed in disappointment.

"What's the matter?"

"I've been having trouble reaching Patrick." In an instant, tears welled in her eyes. She didn't want to cry, her mother would worry.

"He's a busy man, Fleur."

"Yes."

"You can't expect him to hang by the phone twenty-four hours a day."

"I know. I simply wanted to know what time he was leaving for the airport." Fleur's throat tightened with emotion. "I haven't heard from him since he was in Ireland last week."

"Well, I wouldn't worry, darling. I'm sure there's some explanation."

"Being so far away it's easy to panic, you know? I keep thinking something has happened to him."

"Of course, it's natural. Now, I was just phoning to see if you were coming around to help with the decorations tomorrow. Susannah delivered the boxes this morning and—"

"Mum, I'm sorry to interrupt but do you remember me ever mentioning the village where Patrick's parents live?"

"Um...no, sorry. Why?"

"I thought to ring information and get their number just in case Patrick has had an accident or something."

"Oh, I see. Well, have you tried his restaurants? Perhaps they know something."

Fleur slapped her forehead. "I didn't think of them. Lord, I'm dumb."

"Well getting yourself into a panic is a bit silly, darling. Now, about tomorrow..."

As her mother rambled on about flowers and glasses and silk ribbons, Fleur rummaged through her bag for her diary. Once found, she flicked through the pages looking for the

Whitby restaurant number. She didn't have the number for the Manchester one, but the staff in Whitby would give it to her. Finally she found what she needed and then switched her attention back to her mother. "Look, Mum, I have to go."

"What about tomorrow. I need you to collect—"

"I'll be at the house early, I promise. But I have to use the phone. Bye." Fleur hung up and then winced at what she had done. Hanging up on her mother was a capital offense. Oh well, if she got in touch with Patrick it would be worth it, and she'd say sorry to her mother tomorrow.

The ringing went on in her ear for what felt like hours but was only seconds. At last someone picked the phone up and a soft, sensual voice said hello. Angela.

Her sixth sense or womanly instinct put her on alert.

"Hi, Angela. It's Fleur Stanthorpe. Is Patrick there by any chance?"

"Oh, hello, Fleur. I thought you had gone back to Australia?"

"I have. I am." Fleur cursed silently. Why couldn't she speak properly in front of this woman of all people? "I mean I'm calling from Australia."

"Oh. I see."

Fleur took a deep breath. While in England she'd not really felt threatened by Angela's apparent interest in Patrick, but now, being so far away did nothing to help her insecurities. "Is Patrick there?"

"No, he isn't. Sorry."

"Do you know if he's going to be at the restaurant at any time tonight?"

"No idea, sorry. Is it important?"

"Well, yes it is actually." Fleur wanted to swear badly. The bloody woman was enjoying this.

Angela's voice became flippant as though she was talking to someone of no importance. "Did he leave you his mobile number? I know he doesn't give it to everyone..."

Gripping the phone, Fleur wanted to scream at her that of course she had his numbers, but instead spoke in a lighter, sweeter tone. "Naturally, being his *girlfriend*, I have his numbers but I thought I would catch him at the restaurant tonight. The time differences play havoc with our arrangements." *There, stick that, you cow.*

"Well, he's been away. The new manager might know more though. Shall I get him for you?"

New manager? That threw her completely. She felt so out of touch.

"Um. Yes please." She waited for several minutes before a man's voice sounded in her ear.

"This is Luke Higgins. May I help you?"

Once again Fleur explained what she wanted, but the manager could only reveal that Mr. Donnelly was away on business and no, at this stage, he didn't know when he'd return.

After disconnecting, Fleur flopped down onto the sofa. If Patrick were ill, then the manager would know about it. Patrick had made no mention of a new manager for the Whitby Donnelly's. Why wouldn't he tell her?

Mainly because you haven't properly talked in two weeks.

She scowled at the blank screen of her mobile. No messages. It was so frustrating she could scream. In a last ditch attempt to save her sanity, she started up her computer to check her emails. When eventually they downloaded into her inbox, she nearly had a heart attack on seeing Patrick's name. Her hand shook as she guided the mouse over to click on his email.

Hi Babe.

Just a quick email to let you know that I'm away on business for a few days.

I've booked my flight, but it was difficult. All seats gone for the 23rd. I should have booked weeks ago but got tied up. (Yes, I know you told me to do it much earlier, but it's been crazy here) Sorry. But I did manage to get one of the last seats left on a Qantas flight for the 24th. I land in Sydney at 6:30 pm.

Miss you.

Love You.

Patrick.

PS. I can't wait to see you in a few days. I'll be the one coming out of the arrivals area with a rose between my teeth.

The last bit made Fleur smile. She put her hand over her mouth as tears slipped down her cheeks. He was coming.

Bing Crosby's "White Christmas" filled the living room of Fleur's parents' home, accompanied by Fleur's off-key singing. Nothing made Christmas more exciting than listening to this song and putting up the Christmas tree. What did it matter that Australian Christmases were hot and held in the middle of summer and nothing like those in the cold, snowy Northern hemisphere countries.

She stepped back to admire her handiwork and nodded in satisfaction. The tree looked great in the red and gold decorations she'd chosen to use. Her mother had placed all the presents to one side for her to arrange underneath and she did that now—though she couldn't help but gently shake the boxes that had her name on them.

Next on her list of jobs was to decorate the lounge room in a mirror image of how the marquee would eventually look, which at this moment was being erected in the backyard by the men from the marquee company, along with a collection of the bride and groom's family members, neighbors and Charlie's football mates.

As Fleur hung long flower ropes and white satin ribbons for decoration, she could hear from the kitchen a babble of voices. Her mum, Susannah and Susannah's mother, Helen, were talking, and no doubt giving last minute directions to the caterers.

A large box full of wedding decorations sat on the floor near the sofa. She'd been instructed to hang long ropes of intertwined white material flowers and green ivy across the ceiling and on the opposite diagonal she must hang swathes of white satin. Grabbing one end of a flower rope, Fleur climbed the stepladder and pinned it into the cornice. Glancing down she realized that the other end of the rope had got tangled around the stepladder. "Bugger!"

The front door opened and she heard Charlie's voice. "Charlie, can you come here a minute, please?" She glanced over her shoulder. "I need a hand to put this—"

The words died in her throat, as standing in the middle of the living room was Patrick. Her skin tingled, her heart somersaulted and her stomach clenched all at the same time.

"Hello, sweetheart." His beautiful blue eyes glowed with love and he gave her the sexiest grin imaginable.

She smiled through her tears as he stepped towards her. It seemed incredible that after all these weeks of waiting he'd arrived without her even knowing. “You’re not meant to be here until tomorrow evening.”

He raised his eyebrows. “I can always go and come back tomorrow then.”

“No.” She flung herself off the ladder and into his arms. He smothered her face with kisses. She held him and kissed him back with equal intensity. “I can’t believe you’re here.”

“Nor me.”

“I’ve missed you so much.

Patrick kissed the tip of her nose. “Not half as bad as I’ve missed you. It’s been awful.”

She ran her hands over his shoulders, gazing at him as if he wasn’t real. The hard feel of him beneath her fingers reassured her. “How did I bear being without you?” she murmured between kisses.

“I think we only just managed it, don’t you?” He grinned.

“Definitely.” She gave him a smile full of love to show him that he must never doubt her feelings for him.

He stepped back a little, though still keeping her within the circle of his arms, and she realized they had an audience.

Standing behind Charlie was her dad and mum, Susannah and Helen, the caterers and one of the next-door neighbors. Charlie wore a huge grin. “Fleur, you’re gripping him so hard we’ll need a hammer and chisel to prise you off.”

“I’m not letting him go now that he’s here.” She glanced up at Patrick, still not quite believing he stood beside her. Her nerves at seeing him had fled. It felt so right having him here beside her, holding her. “How did you get an earlier flight?”

“I’ve always had this flight booked so I could land today. I’d arranged it with Charlie and your dad.”

Amazed, Fleur stared wide-eyed at the grinning duo of father and son. "You knew? For how long?"

Charlie puffed himself up importantly. "Oh, weeks. We were all in on it."

Her gaze flew to her mother, and Val stepped forward to hug her. "Do you remember that day we argued?"

Fleur nodded, feeling ill at the thought of that awful day.

"Well, we, your father, Charlie and I decided to take matters into our own hands. I rang Patrick and the two of us had a lovely long chat." Val leaned over and kissed Patrick on the cheek. "We sorted out everything."

"Everything?" Fleur, stunned, could only stare back and forth between Patrick and her mother.

Patrick nodded and kissed her. "I didn't mean to cause you pain, sweetheart, with my lack of communication these last few weeks, but it was all for a good cause. I had to make sure everything was in order before I left."

"To do with the restaurants?"

"Yes, I had to find managers but also for my immigration. I've applied to live permanently in Australia."

"You've what?" The hits just kept coming. She was so happy she was going to explode any moment. "I can't believe this."

"I need a sponsor, my love, that's if you want me." He winked and kissed her again.

She wrapped her arms around him even tighter and kissed him.

Patrick suddenly got down on one knee, and her breath caught in her chest. He fished in the pocket of his leather jacket and pulled out a small velvet box. "Will you marry me?"

Those words... The wonder of them hit her like nothing else. She never expected the power of them. A tear tripped over her lashes. "Yes, absolutely."

Epilogue

Fleur went to stand beside the large bay window. Without moving the curtains she gazed down at the gathering below. White benches were lined up in rows on either side of the red carpet leading to the altar arch. Bouquets of peach and white flowers stood on pedestals around the immediate grounds and swathes of green satin hung above the benches from tree to tree. Her heart swelled with love, pride and excitement—with just a hint of nerves.

She picked out family friends and the staff from the bakery, all dressed in their finery. The afternoon sunlight reflected from the crystal champagne flutes that the guests were holding. People were still arriving and wandering around the gardens of the historical home they'd hired for today's event. She smiled as Patrick's parents came into view from under a large pine tree. They headed straight for her mother and instantly began chatting. It pleased her and Patrick so much that they had managed to fly out from Ireland to Australia for this special day. It mustn't have been easy for them to know that Patrick would spend much of his time far away from them, but not once did they make her feel guilty for taking their son away to the other side of the world.

Her mother looked sensational in a long dress of dark blue. She looked relaxed and younger than her fifty-six years. Fleur was pleased that finally she could give her mum a break from worrying over her. She was quite content to stay in one place now, just as long as that place included Patrick.

Then, she saw him. The one who made her heart pound. The one who made her world a better place. Patrick looked incredible in top hat and tails. She remembered his initial hesitancy when she first mentioned him wearing them, but thankfully he'd come around to her way of thinking. Their extraordinary day had been organized with a theme of old-world class.

Her eyes misted as she gazed down at him. He looked happy, if a little tense as he shook hands with the male guests and kissed the women. That he would soon be declaring his love for her in front of everyone important to them made her feel so wonderfully happy and safe. She couldn't believe her luck in being loved so deeply by such a fantastic man.

"You look so lovely."

"I still can't believe it's real."

Fleur turned and smiled at the gushing Susannah and Rachel, who held Courtney's hand. "I can't quite believe it myself. You all look so wonderful." Her gaze lingered over every detail of their emerald satin bridesmaid dresses. The strapless gowns shimmered to the floor and when they walked, she could just see their silver shoes peeping out from beneath.

Susannah wiped away a tear. "I haven't stopped crying over my own wedding yet and here I am at another." She quickly crossed the room and kissed Fleur's cheek. "I'm just going to fix my makeup."

"Again?" Fleur laughed.

Once Susannah had left the room, Rachel stepped closer and Fleur bent to adjust Courtney's emerald sash around the waist of her white satin flower girl's dress. "Doesn't she look gorgeous?"

Rachel nodded, her smile full of pride. "We both are still in shock, I think. It's amazing that we're in Australia, but to be a part of your wedding is even more surreal."

"Patrick and I couldn't have this day without you in it."

Rachel hugged Fleur to her and kissed her cheek. "Thank you. Meeting you changed my life. I have a business, a brighter future for me and for Courtney and, best of all, I have you as my dearest friend."

The tears welled in Fleur's eyes. "Lord, don't make me cry. I'll ruin my makeup like Susannah."

They laughed and then the door opened. Fleur smiled as her father hesitated in the doorway, looking splendid in top hat and tails.

Rachel grabbed Courtney's hand and headed for the door. "I'll check to see if they're ready for us."

John walked further into the room, his smile stretching wide. "Well, my darling, you take my breath away."

Fleur blinked back her tears and glanced down at the magnificent dress she wore. The white tulle skirt over an underskirt of white satin sprayed out a good meter and a half. The whale-boned bodice fitted perfectly to her shape and she gently touched the sprig of lavender tucked inside the top of it. She grinned up at her dad. "You don't look too bad yourself."

He straightened the lapels of his jacket and raised his chin, pretending to be superior. "Indeed I do, my dear."

Chuckling, she touched his silk cravat. "Thank you for this day, Dad."

He kissed her cheek. "No, thank you. Your mother and I are very proud of you."

"I bet you both thought this day would never come."

"We had our moments." He laughed.

Rachel poked her head around the doorway. "They're ready for us now."

Fleur took a deep breath as her dad held out his arm for her. "Ready?"

Her heart was lodged somewhere in her throat but she smiled and nodded. Oh yes, she was more than ready. "Yes."

They walked out of the main dressing room, into the hallway and down the main staircase to the foyer. The noise of the guests filtered back to them and Fleur's nerves grew. Rachel, Courtney and Susannah formed a line in front of them and then suddenly a waiter appeared beside Fleur.

"Oh, I'm terribly sorry, Miss Stanthorpe, but the groom's father, Mr. Donnelly, wants to know if there's any Guinness being served?"

Fleur hid a grin, as at the same time the music started signaling their arrival. She smiled at the young waiter. "Yes, there's Guinness for him. Have a glass ready for him after the ceremony."

The waiter looked startled but nodded and quickly disappeared.

"Guinness?" her father whispered out the side of his mouth.

Fleur winked at him as they headed for the red carpet and the man she loved who stood there waiting for her. "Well, it is St Patrick's Day after all."

About the Author

Anne Whitfield lives in the beautiful Southern Highlands area of New South Wales, Australia. She is married with three children. She writes historical fiction and contemporary novels and short stories. The areas she has set her books include both Yorkshire England and Australia.

To learn more about Anne Whitfield, please visit http://www.annewhitfield.com Send an email to Anne Whitfield at AnneWhitfield46@hotmail.com or join her Yahoo! group http://groups.yahoo.com/group/AnneWhitfield_Newsletter/.

Look for these titles

Now Available

Kitty McKenzie
Kitty McKenzie's Land

Suddenly left as the head of the family, Kitty McKenzie must find her inner strength to keep her family together against the odds.

Kitty McKenzie

Evicted from their resplendent home in the fashionable part of York after her parents' deaths, Kitty must fight the legacy of bankruptcy and homelessness to secure a home for her and her siblings.

Through sheer willpower and determination she grabs opportunities with both hands from working on a clothes and rag stall in the market to creating a teashop for the wealthy. Her road to happiness is fraught with obstacles of hardship and despair, but she refuses to let her dream of a better life for her family die. She soon learns that love and loyalty brings its own reward.

Kitty McKenzie's Land
© 2006 Anne Whitfield

1866

Kitty McKenzie path has taken her from the slums of York to the inhospitable bush of colonial Australia. Yet, when she believes her dreams will never be attained, she is shown that sometimes life can be even better than what you wish for.

Kitty McKenzie is gifted land in the far north of New South Wales. Life at the northern property is full of hardships as she learns how to become a successful landowner.

However, Kitty's strength of will and belief in herself gives her the courage most women of her time never realize they have. A decided thorn in her side is the arrogant and patronizing Miles Grayson, owner of the adjourning run. He wants her gone so he can have her land, but he wants *her* even more.

CPSIA information can be obtained at www.ICGtesting.com
Printed in the USA
LVOW050108190612

286717LV00002B/117/A

9 781599 985718